"So you're afra
with the boss?" he said.

"I'm not afraid of anything," she snapped.

"Really?"

He moved closer, and she backed right into the hallway wall until there was nowhere else for her to go. Her arms shifted to a defensive stance folded over her chest. She took that stance often enough that he was beginning to read the warning signs. But it wasn't going to stop him, not this time. He pressed even closer. "Are you sure you're not afraid of me? Of what I make you feel?" he whispered, lowering his face closer to hers.

"You don't make me feel anything," she said, but her breath was soft and airy.

"I don't make you feel like you want to be made love to? Like you want my hands on your body, my lips on yours?"

She shook her head, her lips clamping tight as she swallowed.

"Prove it," he said, touching his lips lightly to hers. "Prove you're not afraid."

His lips slid along hers once more.

"How?" she breathed against him.

"Kiss me. Just this once, Tate, kiss me."

Books by A.C. Arthur

Harlequin Kimani Romance

Love Me Like No Other
A Cinderella Affair
Guarding His Body
Second Chance, Baby
Defying Desire
Full House Seduction
Summer Heat
Sing Your Pleasure
Touch of Fate
Winter Kisses
Desire a Donovan
Surrender to a Donovan

ARTIST C. ARTHUR

was born and raised in Baltimore, Maryland, where she currently resides with her husband and three children. An active imagination and a love for reading encouraged her to begin writing in high school, and she hasn't stopped since.

Determined to bring a new edge to romance, she continues to develop intriguing plots, racy characters and fresh dialogue—thus keeping readers on their toes! Visit her website at www.acarthur.net.

SURRENDER
To A
DONOVAN

A.C. ARTHUR

This book is dedicated to all the readers
who have taken the Donovan family into your hearts. I am
so grateful to you for allowing me to share these stories.

Recycling programs
for this product may
not exist in your area.

ISBN-13: 978-0-373-86276-4

SURRENDER TO A DONOVAN

Dear Reader,

You've already met Dion of the Miami Donovans, and now you'll get to see his younger brother fall in love.

Sean is the younger brother, the more serious and business-minded Donovan, with a heart of gold that he's been waiting to share with the right woman. Enter Tate Dennison, a single mother with a troubled past. I love writing stories with children because I feel they add another dimension to what's emotionally at stake when two people fall in love. Little Briana weaves an impenetrable knot around Sean's heart from the start, making it hard for Tate to resist him.

I hope you'll enjoy this segment of the Donovans.

Happy reading,

AC

Prologue

He never dreamed, at least not this vividly. But he felt everything as if she were rubbing her hands over his skin right at this very moment. He tasted the sweetness of her lips on his and caught himself puckering with the thought.

With a groan and a sigh, Sean tossed in bed, flopping over on his back, one arm on his bare chest, the other on the pillow above his head. Okay, it was a dream. He'd awakened and now it was over. It was still night, so he closed his eyes once more and prayed that, whoever she was, the temptress did not invade the remainder of his rest....

She eased her way toward him, on her hands and knees. His body was on full alert. She did not speak, didn't really have to. Sean knew what she wanted, because he wanted the same thing. He reached for her, held her hips as she pushed one leg over to straddle him. Her breasts were full and heavy as he palmed them, her sighs music to his ears as she arched to his touch. When she came down over him, her center sucking his arousal deep, deep inside, he let out a low moan.

She moved on top of him, creating a rhythm that brushed along his body like fine silk. His hips joined in as if this were their routine. She rode him hard, with an uninhibited desire that pushed him closer to the brink. And when she let her head fall back, her mouth open as a scream of pleasure echoed through the room, Sean felt his own release brewing. With rapid pumps, he emptied himself into her.

As she collapsed onto his chest and he wrapped his arms around her, he felt like he'd lost something else to her as well.

The next time his eyes opened it was morning, his body was covered in sweat, and his heart was beating frantically in his chest.

In the shower he berated himself for having a schoolboy's sex dream. Dressing for work, he vowed to make more time in his busy life for women. Either that or he'd end up in the nuthouse like his great uncle Javier, who died with one of the mental hospital's nurses on top of him.

Chapter 1

Numbers didn't lie.

Sean Donovan had learned that lesson early in life—somewhere around third grade, when he thought he could change the grade on his report card from a 75 to a 95. His father, Bruce Donovan, had been skeptical about the one grade on the report card that had been made in blue ink versus the remaining ones in black ink. The conference with his teacher had sealed Sean's fate, as Mr. Crutcheon had meticulously added up every one of Sean's test grades in his class. Then he divided and came up with the average grade. It was a 75.

"Numbers don't lie, son," his father had said to him with his solemn, you're-in-big-trouble voice.

Those three words had stuck with him all his life, and Sean had never tried anything as deceitful as that again. Luckily for him, his mother, Janean, had selected his punishment instead of his father. Janean's mind leaned more toward the manual labor type of punishment, while Bruce was standing stern on the corporal punishment ladder. It was his older brother, Dion, who was usually on the receiving end of their dad's punishment. Sean had never envied his big brother that.

As a Donovan, Sean was a descendent of men who began their fortune in oil refineries and then branched out into such areas as the military, casino ownership, real estate, mass media, and the one that had given the family name worldwide attention—philanthropy. His father was one of six brothers whose families stretched across the United States, and their father came from a family of four brothers and two sisters. To put it mildly, the Donovans were deep. They were well-known and respected. Which Sean sometimes thought of as a blessing and a curse.

While he loved his job as managing editor at *Infinity* magazine, a division of DNT, the Donovan Multimedia Network, there were days when he wished he would have done something else with his life. He'd gone to Columbia, his father's alma mater, and had majored in English with a minor in finance—even though he really had a deep love of history. That love probably wouldn't have lasted into a career, but sometimes, actually—days like today—he wondered what if.

Sean's office at *Infinity* was huge, located on the corner of the third floor of the Excalibur Business Center, which was owned by DNT. The walls were a rich mahogany color with chocolate-tone carpet lining the floors. The furniture was heavy and gave the room an old law firm feel. It could be considered somber and professional. The somber part would not be an exaggeration.

Sean held a piece of paper in one hand, while his finger skimmed down a column of numbers on another sheet that lay on the desk. Numbers do not lie, he said to himself once more.

Infinity was picking up major distribution numbers, which was a good thing. But so was *Onyx, Infinity*'s rival magazine.

Onyx was owned by Sabine Ravenell, and it provided entertainment news about African American celebrities. Just last year they'd begun an up-and-coming segment that boosted their sales. Now, they were neck and neck with *Infinity*.

Actually, he thought, dropping the paper onto his desk and dragging his hands down his face, *Infinity* still had a lead on *Onyx*. But not big enough to suit Sean's standards.

"Bad news, huh?" Dion Donovan said, coming into Sean's office and closing the door behind him.

Sean had been so deep in concentration that he hadn't even heard the door open. Then again, his older brother rarely knocked on his door anyway, and Gayle, Sean's assistant, had long since stopped announcing him. He never gave her time to do so before barging into the office.

"Let's just say it's not good," Sean replied, sitting back in his chair. He pinched the bridge of his nose. "What are you doing here so late?" A glance at the clock on his desk told him it was past seven.

"Come on, man. You know I don't punch a clock around here." Dion had taken a seat, propping one ankle up on his knee and sitting back in the chair.

He looked a lot like their father, with his tall stature and serious dark eyes. But that's where the similarities ended. Dion was the epitome of good looks. He was every girl's fantasy, with his broad, sculpted body and chiseled face. In fact, Dion was considered the gorgeous brother, while Sean had succumbed to the comments that he should be a cover model with his so-called quiet and sophisticated good looks. He didn't much care for those comments. And to be frank, the attention made him uncomfortable. Dion, on the other hand, was more than content with all the fanfare his looks garnered.

"You don't punch a clock, but you've got a beautiful woman at home waiting for you. That should be enough to have you running for the elevator at closing time."

Three months ago, Dion had announced that he was in love with Lyra Anderson, the woman who had grown up with them. One month after that, Dion and Lyra were married in an intimate ceremony at the Big House—Sean and Dion's parents' house in Key Biscayne, Florida.

To Sean, Lyra was his little sister, and she had been since the day his mother had brought her home saying she was spending the night. Lyra's mother, who had just recently died in a car accident, had been on drugs and couldn't properly care for Lyra. So Janean Donovan had done the honors. But for Dion, Lyra had not been a little sister—she'd been more like the other half to his whole. Sean could see that in his brother's eyes each time he mentioned Lyra.

"She's working late, too. I'm picking her up in half an hour and then we're going out to dinner. You want to join us?"

Sean traced a finger along his chin. He needed to

shave, he thought as he felt the usually lightly trimmed hair there. "Last time I checked, being a third wheel was no fun."

"You're not a third wheel. You're family. Plus, we can talk about what's bothering you."

He shook his head. "Nothing but the usual. Trying to keep a step ahead of *Onyx*."

"Yeah? Is Ravenell still riding you about selling?"

He nodded. "She is."

"But she doesn't call me or Dad," Dion said, leaning back to let his finger run against his chin as well.

To an outsider, the two similar men rubbing their goatees in the same way might have been strange. To them, it was the norm. Sean and Dion were very close, as were the other members of the Donovan family that resided in Miami with them. It was no wonder they had similar mannerisms when they spent so much time together.

Sean shrugged. "I don't know what's in her head."

Dion chuckled.

"What?" Sean asked quizzically. "Private joke?"

"Man, how can you know so much about numbers and sales and distribution and know absolutely nothing about females?"

"I know that she's working my nerves by constantly asking to buy *Infinity*. I've told her a million times we're not interested in selling."

"She keeps asking you because she's got a thing for you," Dion said, his eyebrows hitching up and down as if he were waiting for Sean to catch on.

When Dion's mind wasn't on *Infinity,* it was most likely on sleeping with women. Or at least, that had been the case before Lyra returned from L.A.

And now that Sean knew what his brother was thinking, he had to frown. "Then I'd hate to break the bad news to her," he said. "Ravenell is not my type."

Dion laughed so hard Sean thought he would fall out of the chair. Sabine Ravenell was likely in her early forties, but that was a modest guess on his part. In her younger years she'd been an actress and had a couple of adult movies that garnered her some fame. This put her name on the charts and built her fan base, which consisted mainly of college boys looking for the next best thing to a *Playboy* magazine to keep them company at night. Now, she still had the vivacious and bawdy attitude of a woman of her background. Did she have a thing for Sean? Probably. Did he give a damn? Of course not!

"Right," Dion said, still trying to regain his composure.

"But her sales are looking good," he said contemplatively.

"How'd you get your hands on her sales figures?"

It was Sean's turn to smile now. "I have my connections."

Dion nodded. "Yeah, I guess the same way she seems to know what's going on in our camp. Listen, the real reason I stopped by was to ask if you've had a chance to speak to Parker."

Parker Donovan was their cousin, son of Reginald and Carolyn. Uncle Reginald had always had his hands more into DNT, so it made sense that his sons would follow in his footsteps. Parker did a lot of scouting for new programs, while Savian focused on upcoming business ventures and spotlighting entrepreneurs. Regan, the youngest of Uncle Reginald's children, and the only girl, worked at *Infinity,* heading up the fashion and entertainment portions of the magazine. She, along with Camille, who was married to Adam Donovan of the Las Vegas branch of the family, were currently developing a reality TV show that would center around the life of a fashion designer. Meanwhile, under Savian's watchful eye, the men were charged with developing a show that would transform *Infinity* magazine's print success to television.

"I had a message from him when I came back from lunch, but I haven't had a chance to call him back."

"You actually took a lunch?" Dion asked with another raise of his brows.

Sean was getting tired of his brother's assumptions and innuendos. "What does Parker want? Since you're in here at this time of night asking about him, it must be important."

"He wants to talk to you about adding the relationship column to the magazine show. Says the online version is getting lots of traffic."

That was true. Sean had seen that for the past three months there had been a rise in the mail coming in for the "Ask Jenny" column. Then eight weeks ago, after their monthly meeting, he'd decided to expand the column from its quarter page to a full page to see what would happen. The change had gone over well.

"There's a good following there. Do you read the column?" Sean was curious, since his brother usually kept his finger on every inch of the magazine. As editor-in-chief of *Infinity,* it was his job to know everything that went into the magazine as well as the feedback they received.

"I've read it. Jenny sounds like she's been through a

lot—knows the ropes," Dion said with a slight chuckle. "It's just what women in the twenty-five to thirty-five demographic are looking for. Honest and brash."

Sean was nodding as he listened to his brother, thinking about the last "Ask Jenny" column he'd read recently. "Real," he said. "That's the tone I picked up when I read it. She sounds like a real woman, with real issues of her own."

"Right. So let's think about how that might play out on television. Dr. Phil and Dr. Oz have shows—why shouldn't we look into putting our own relationship guru out there?"

"It definitely has merit," Sean agreed.

"Good," Dion said, standing. "So I'll tell Parker you're going to talk to her, and we'll met up later this week to see if it's something to really look into."

"Wait a minute. I'm going to talk to who?"

"Jenny, or whatever her name is that writes the column. Is it really Jenny?" Dion asked with a quizzical look on his face. "That's probably not smart to have her real name out there."

Sean was standing now, pulling his suit jacket from the back of his chair and slipping his arms inside. "No, her name's not Jenny. And why aren't you or Parker talking to her? Better yet, why not just call her into a meeting with all of us?"

Dion was at the door when he turned to give Sean an appeasing look. "She's not going to bite you, Sean. You know, if you weren't my brother, I might start to question this aversion you have to women."

Sean tossed a teasing jab at his brother, his fist landing on Dion's biceps. "You know better," he said. "I can talk to women just fine. I do it on a daily basis."

"Yeah, but those women aren't analyzing the good, bad and ugly truths about men. Good luck with that one," he said, then walked through the door.

"Man, I'm a Donovan," Sean said, following his brother out to the elevators. "I don't need luck."

Chapter 2

Dear Jenny,

I'm confused. I am a 32-year-old woman with two sons living with my 35-year-old boyfriend, who has three children from a previous relationship that also live with us. I work a full-time job and take care of the house and the children. My boyfriend is an entrepreneur—trying to open his own barber shop. We've been together for ten years.

I want to get married. He doesn't understand why what we have is not enough. I want commitment and love and stability for our family. Especially since I don't mind taking care of his kids as well as the ones we share together. I'm not even complaining about having to pay the bulk of our household bills myself. I am a Christian and have

*been taking all our kids to church for years, but
my boyfriend never comes with us.*

*There is this life I want with a family and a
household built on Christian love and respect.
Then there's this feeling that I'm still shacking up,
and as my girlfriends keep reminding me, "settling" for less because he obviously does not want
to commit to me.*

*Last Valentine's Day my boyfriend proposed. I
was so excited. I couldn't wait to show everyone
the diamond ring he gave me. I immediately went
out and bought wedding books and started writing down my plans for the wedding. But when I
asked him about setting a date he said he wanted
to wait. It's been more than a year, and we're
still waiting. Problem is, I don't know what we're
waiting for.*
Can you help?
In love and confused.

Tate Dennison read the letter for the second time. That
was her process—Nelia, the editorial assistant on this
floor, received the mail and routed each piece to which-
ever staff writer they went to. The second floor of the
Excalibur Building was dedicated to the writing staff
of *Infinity* magazine. Once Nelia had gone through the
mail, she brought Tate her stack. Tate then separated
the letters into two piles—male and female questions—
because she needed a different type of focus when answering each letter.

Was this the way she thought she'd be using the journalism degree she'd received from Morgan State Uni-
versity in Maryland? Of course not, but it paid the bills.

It was nearing five-thirty in the afternoon and already she'd answered four letters, attended a staff writers' meeting and let the graphics director talk her ear off for about an hour. The one thing she hadn't done was answer her cell phone again. It had started ringing around noon and continued every half hour. The first couple of times she'd answered the unknown number, but then she grew tired of the hang-ups and turned the ringer to vibrate. Still, she'd kept an eye on the ringing each time, just to be sure it wasn't the day care calling about her daughter.

To say she was tired would have been an understatement. But she was here trying to get more work done. Recently, the magazine had begun printing ten responses in her column per month. But Tate liked to be ahead of the game. She'd learned there was no other way to be.

Because she'd been sitting so long, her feet had started to go numb, so Tate walked to the end of her small office. It probably used to be a closet, she thought, as she skirted around the desk that took up the bulk of her space. Immediately she was face-to-face with the bookshelf that served as an organizer and held all her mail, past columns, along with copies of the letters she'd responded to and pictures of her inspiration squeezed in for good measure.

Her daughter, Briana Suray Dennison, stared back at her with plump cheeks and a tiny toothed grin. She was Tate's star and moon, the reason she'd taken this job and lived in Miami. Briana was basically Tate's reason for living at all. Three months ago, she'd turned two, and her baby chatter was becoming real words like *mama* and *no*. Tate rubbed a finger over the picture, touching the chubby cheeks she loved to kiss and nuzzle. She loved her daughter's smile and the simply joyous look she always had in her eyes. It never failed to make Tate's heart ache.

They were supposed to be a family living happily ever after. And here she was in another state, thousands of miles away from the only family she had left in Maryland. All because of him. No, she corrected herself, moving here and starting over had been her decision. Leaving their family high and dry had been Patrick's. She wouldn't take the blame for what wasn't her fault.

She'd loved him enough to alienate herself from her relatives because they didn't care for him. Had loved him enough to marry him and have his baby. And he'd used her enough to take their savings and all the furniture in their house. Now, nine months after his betrayal, she knew Patrick had never loved her. Their three-year marriage had been a complete lie. And that was fine. She'd resigned herself to that fact, even if Briana's smile reminded her of it every day.

Another reminder of the mess her marriage had turned out to be was writing this damned column. Each morning she came in to another stack of mail, another stack of someone else's relationship problems. And she was the one charged with helping them, when she hadn't been bright enough to see the signs of her own union falling apart. If that wasn't ironic, she didn't know what was.

"Okay, get it together, Dennison," she berated herself. Taking a deep breath, she thought about the letter she'd just read for the second time, about the circumstances and the issues she needed to address.

There were a few. For instance, why was "In love and confused" the only one with gainful employment in this household? What she needed to do was make this boyfriend of hers get a job. "A real job at that," she said aloud and then chuckled and moved on to the next issue.

"Excuse me?"

The deep male voice startled her, and Tate jumped, backed up and slammed her leg into the side of her desk.

"Damn it!" she swore, leaning over to rub her leg and looking up just as the owner of the voice had moved in to catch her.

"Are you all right?" he asked, touching a hand lightly to her shoulder and leaning over slightly to look at the leg she was rubbing.

The full skirt she had on today was a thin paisley material, and it fell between her legs as she rubbed. She realized with a start how much of her thigh she was actually showing and hurriedly pulled it down.

"I'm fine," she said, clearing her throat. "Just fine. Thanks."

"I didn't mean to interrupt," he said. Then he took a step back, stood straight, his eyes trained directly on her.

Tate prayed a big gaping hole would open in the middle of this tiny office floor and swallow her up. Embarrassment spread across her cheeks and down her neck in a heated rush. "How can I help you, Mr. Donovan?"

Yes, she told herself in a stern voice, this was Sean Donovan, the boss, or at least one of the bosses. Tate knew that the Donovans owned *Infinity* and several other media ventures in the Miami area. She'd done her research when she'd applied for the position. He was the younger of the two brothers, the more serious and intense one. Dion was the tall and dangerously hand-some one.

For a minute or two—she couldn't really count right now, but she knew that it seemed like a really long time—he stared at her without speaking.

"Sir?" she prompted, her palms starting to sweat. It was a horrid nervous habit she had. Either her hands sweated or she tripped over her words as if her mind had drawn a blank or her tongue had suddenly become too big for her mouth.

"Call me Sean," he said. If it were possible, his voice sounded even deeper than it had just seconds ago. "And you're Mrs. Dennison?"

"Yes, I'm *Ms.* Dennison." She clapped her lips shut, appalled that she'd actually stressed the *Ms.* "I'm Tate," she said in an effort to correct herself.

"You write the 'Ask Jenny' column?"

She nodded. "I do."

He slipped his hands into his pockets and began looking around her tiny office. He wore a slate-gray suit and a crisp white shirt with an aqua-blue tie. The colors seemed to highlight the buttery tone of his complexion. His head was completely bald, his goatee, full and trim around the bottom half of his face. He was startlingly fine up close, and Tate had to gulp to keep from drooling.

When he stopped looking he turned to her again. Tate shifted from one foot to the other. His stare was intense, as if he were looking straight through to her soul. Her heart hammered, and the palms of her hands sweated profusely.

"Forgive me for staring," he finally said. He looked away only because he was shaking his head. Then his eyes, the warm brown orbs, seemed to zoom right back in on her. "I just pictured the writer of this column a little differently."

A ping of offense vibrated through Tate's chest, and she stood a bit straighter, staring at him with a little more heat than she had been. "I don't understand your meaning."

"I thought you'd be older," he said abruptly.

"Well, I thought you'd be more professional," she said.

Again her lips clamped shut. Tate needed this job, desperately. But she wasn't about to be disrespected for the sake of a paycheck.

His hands came out of his pockets and went up into the air as if she'd been trying to stick him up.

"My fault," he said. There was a twinkle in his eyes, sort of like they were smiling at her. Because his mouth certainly was not. He had the same quizzical expression he'd had when he came in. "I didn't mean anything by that. Just that from reading the column and the advice provided, I assumed the writer was a more mature, experienced woman."

"I assure you, Mr. Donovan, I'm very mature. And experience doesn't make up for common sense. I graduated third in my class with a degree in journalism. I minored in English and have worked on two widely distributed newspapers before coming to *Infinity*. Is there a problem with my work?"

He was shaking his head before she gave him a chance to answer. "Absolutely not. In fact, I was coming to get a feel for the possibilities."

As he spoke he took a step closer to her desk. Now, he didn't look as imposing as he had seconds ago when he'd made his "older" remark. Still, Tate's thighs began to quiver, and her heart beat a quick rhythm in her chest. She flared her fingers, made a move that she hoped seemed natural and wiped her palms on her skirt. "What kind of possibilities?"

"Maybe we can discuss them over dinner," he said, his fingers touching the edge of her desk as he leaned forward slightly.

He was a very tall man. And Tate considered herself tall for a woman, at five feet nine inches. Even so, she had to look up at him, into those eyes that seemed so deep and so assessing.

"No," she snapped. "I can't go to dinner with you." She spoke quickly and moved her arms for some unexplainable reason. The action sent her hands flailing until one smacked into a picture frame on her desk, sending it toppling over.

Of course it would fall right in front of him, and of course he'd pick it up and look at it instead of just setting it upright. Or just leaving it alone and getting out of her office.

"Who's this?" he asked, examining the picture.

Now she was flustered and offended all over again, even though she'd never really calmed down. He'd asked the question as if he deserved an answer. He was her boss, not her man. She took one deep inhale and slowly released the exhale. Okay, she was overreacting. He was only asking a question. Actually, he was asking a lot of questions, but he was the boss, so he could do that.

"It's my daughter," she said, reaching for the picture. It took everything in her not to snatch it from him.

"She's cute. How old is she?"

He didn't give her the picture.

"Two."

He looked up at her, one eyebrow arching as he asked, "And you're not married?"

"You don't have to be married to have a baby. But for the record, yes, I was married to her father when she was born. Now, I'm not." There, he could go now. She touched the edge of the frame in an effort to take it from him.

He held firm.

"So you're divorced?"

"Yes. I mean, almost. I mean, was there something I could do for you, Mr. Donovan?" She snatched the picture from him and wasn't really sure she cared what he thought at that moment.

"You can call me Sean. I'll let you get home to your daughter. But I'd like to talk to you about the column. I'll have my secretary call you with some available times for us to meet."

He'd already stepped back from her desk and was headed to the door when she said, "That's fine."

Her words stopped him, and he turned back to look at her. "Yes, that's very fine," was his parting reply.

Tate dropped into her chair, clutching the picture of Briana to her chest and let out another deep breath. That was a tension-filled meeting. A confusing meeting. A "damn-oh-damn, that man is too damned fine" meeting.

Chapter 3

They'd tried mashed potatoes for dinner. That had gone over well, Tate thought with a smirk. At two years old, Briana already had plenty of personality. And along with that personality came a pickiness with foods. Tate had mistakenly assumed that any type of baby food would do as long as she didn't have an allergic reaction to anything. She was sadly mistaken.

Briana did not like any of the green vegetables. The result was green splatters all over the kitchen floor, the high chair and whatever Tate was wearing that day. Miraculously, Briana herself remained untouched by the ill-smelling guck. Tonight Tate had tried another tactic—she'd whipped up some homemade mashed potatoes and mixed them with the ingredients from her mother's chicken soup recipe. Briana wasn't a fan of the broth, so Tate's plan was to see if she'd eat the chicken and vegetables if they were submersed in another texture. The first few spoonfuls had gone okay, so Tate had relaxed and let herself enjoy the bonding time with her daughter.

Then Briana made a face that originally Tate thought was funny but soon became concerned about. She looked like she wanted to cry but couldn't quite get it out. Afraid she might be choking, Tate hurriedly scooped her out of the high chair and began patting her back. Maybe her windpipe had been clogged. But as soon as Tate began patting Briana's back, there was an explosion—both from her mouth and inside her diaper. It had taken the last hour and a half to clean all of Briana and put her to bed and clean the kitchen.

Now Tate was ready for some "me time." Only there was nothing to do. She'd thought of running a hot bath and soaking with a good book to read, but the thought of going back into the bathroom made her temples throb. Opting for a quick shower instead, she entered her bedroom and was about to switch on the television when something caught her eye. Tate looked toward the two windows on the side of the room. The blinds were pulled up to the halfway mark, and navy blue valances that matched the comforter on her bed covered the top.

Before she could stop herself, Tate yelped at the sight of a masked face pressed against the window. Moving quickly to her nightstand, she picked up the softball bat she kept against the wall between the stand and the bed. She'd played second base in high school and now gripped the bat in her hands as if she were ready to hit a home run. Nervous legs carried her closer to the windows, but as she approached she felt a tingle of relief. There was no one there. Hurriedly, she pushed the blinds farther upward to check the locks on each window and then pulled on the blind strings until they were completely unwound and the edges were dangling on the floor. She could do without sunlight tomorrow morning.

With a sigh and a nervous chuckle, she berated herself for overreacting. As tired as she was, she could have seen sheep running around her room. She went to the television and turned it on.

Tate had only been in Miami for six months and had just recently gone over to the dark side and ordered cable. So far, so good.

She climbed into the full-sized bed she'd finally purchased after sleeping on a futon for the first five months of her time here. The first thing that caught her eye on the screen was that vaguely transparent DNT logo at the bottom left of the screen. Donovan Network Television.

"Can't get away from them, huh?" she said fluffing her pillows and positioning them so she could sit up and watch television until her eyes demanded she sleep.

Tate never slept well, hadn't since the last night Patrick was with her. She convinced herself it was because she was in a strange town and didn't know anybody. What if Briana cried out in the middle of the night? She had a baby monitor in her bedroom, and the transmitter was hooked up in Briana's room. Still, she couldn't shake the edgy feeling of being in a new place.

She had no idea what she was watching on television, but she didn't change the channel. The program went to a commercial with a gorgeous woman wearing a stunning dress. She was on a fashion runway, and then the camera panned over to the guests of the fashion show and a smiling Regan Donovan. Tate knew her from work. Regan was the only female Donovan working at the magazine. She was as pretty as the model, especially when she smiled, which she was doing right now as she announced a new show coming to DNT.

"With photography by Lyra Donovan and judging by Camille Davis Donovan of CK Davis Designs, one lucky woman's dreams will come true. *The Fashionista* promises to bring you everything you're looking for in reality television—beautiful women, great clothes, sexy men and drama, drama, drama!"

Music followed Regan's pitch with the date and time of the show's kickoff running across the bottom of the screen.

Tate smiled, wondering just how it would feel to have her own dreams come true. Growing up she'd dreamed of going to college, getting a good job as a writer and having a family. It wasn't much, but it was her dream. And once upon a time she'd had it.

Then she didn't.

And that pissed her off. She snapped the television off and plopped down in the bed, pulling the sheets up over her shoulder. But when Tate closed her eyes, she didn't see the normal memories from her past. The usual aching in her chest at what had been lost or what had never been hers in the first place wasn't there. All of that was replaced by one set of intense brown eyes, one solemn look and the name of one man: Sean Donovan.

A glass of red wine in hand, Sean sat in a lounge chair watching the city skyline at sunset. He was on the wraparound patio of his penthouse condo in downtown Miami's Marina Blue. After taking a sip from his glass, he set it on the arm of the chair and could almost hear his mother scolding him. There were two things about Janean Donovan that were a definite: she loved her family fiercely, and she demanded respect of people and their belongings, which she saw as blessings from the good Lord. The latter were her exact words.

The fabric was some type of leather, but not really leather. And that was on purpose, even though for the price he paid, Sean couldn't figure out why. All he knew was that his mother had picked out the charcoal-gray set, which consisted of a six-section sofa and a solo chair and ottoman. The color complemented the smooth cement finish of the patio and its four-foot walls. The tinted glass doors that lead to this outside oasis were in a dark gray tone as well.

Admittedly, he loved this space. It was perhaps his favorite of the entire condo because it was so peaceful. He could sit out here and actually hear himself think. Or he could sit out here and hear absolutely nothing because it was so relaxing. The inside of the house wasn't his absolute favorite. Not because of the décor, because again, Janean had made sure he had the best designer in Miami. And while his mother had tried to make a lot of the decisions for him, she allowed herself to be nudged when he was really adamant about something. He was her youngest child, so it had been a little harder for her to let go of him when he'd moved out. Even though that was every bit of five years ago.

Tonight his mood was somber, which wasn't abnormal for Sean. He was the quieter of Bruce Donovan's sons, the reserved and serious one. It was true that he preferred to be alone the majority of the time, but there were times, more lately than he cared to admit, that he craved company. He'd turned thirty last year and since that time had been seriously thinking about his future.

Along those lines, work had been really on his mind lately. *Infinity* was his baby. It was his father's creation, and Dion ran the magazine with his smooth expertise. But this magazine meant something to Sean he doubted his family could ever imagine. He was in control of distribution and the daily supervision of the writing staff. He kept a close eye on their bottom line, making sure they were always operating in the black. This job was his purpose in life, the one he'd seemed born into. His father and his brother were counting on him to do his very best at all times. And so that's what he tried to do.

But Sabine was moving in on them. Her distribution was way up, and her sales were getting dangerously close to *Infinity*'s. And she was trying to get close to him. Even though there was definitely no interest there. She was older than he was and carried it well, but her tone could become vicious in mere seconds, and she wasn't worth his time.

Just like that, a mental picture of another woman appeared. She was about five feet five with a pretty caramel complexion and eyes that he presumed held every emotion she felt at any given time. She'd been flustered when he was there, then a tad annoyed. Tate Dennison was definitely not what he'd pictured when he'd thought of the "Ask Jenny" column. She was too damned pretty to be holed up in that small office all day answering questions about someone else's relationship problems. She should be out enjoying a fulfilling relationship of her own.

Then he'd seen the picture of her daughter and a few things had clicked into place. What he hadn't seen was a wedding ring on her finger, and that added to his assessment of her. Single mother, bitter female, believes she knows the secret behind every man and is out to expose them.

He could find that unappealing, but he didn't. He could be just a little bit angry at the woman who took her time to write detailed articles on why a woman should ditch a man that wasn't treating her right. Yet, he found himself more than a little intrigued.

The doorbell rang, which Sean would normally consider a distraction. Tonight, however, he thought it might actually be more like a sign that he should stop thinking about his mysterious columnist.

Pulling the patio doors closed behind him, he took his glass of wine with him as he walked through the living room and down the steps to the foyer. When he finally opened the door, it wasn't a huge surprise to see his cousin Parker. In addition to the fact that he lived about ten minutes from Sean, Parker was a free spirit. He worked hard and played even harder, and he never stayed still long enough to grow entanglements—as some might call women with definite ideas of what they wanted from a man.

"What's up, man? You didn't return my call," Parker said as he entered.

"Right, my apologies. You flying solo tonight?" Sean asked as he closed the door and followed his cousin to the kitchen.

Parker had the appetite of an entire football team, or at least that's what they'd all thought since they were kids, when he'd been able to eat more than all of them combined.

"Nah, I'm heading to pick up this new lady."

Sean's kitchen was straight down the foyer, past the steps to the left and the bathroom and first floor bedroom to the right. The walls were painted a muted beige while the contemporary look of cherrywood cabinets and stainless-steel appliances added a bit of splash.

Parker was already poking his head into the Sub-Zero refrigerator.

"Jaydon seems to think I should meet this girl."

Sean pulled out a chair and sat at the island watching his cousin pull out a beer and a piece of sweet potato pie left over from last Sunday's family dinner at the Big House. That's what they called his parents' home in Key Biscayne. The entire family, or at least the Miami portion of the Donovans, usually gathered there on Sunday afternoons, after church, for dinner.

"Your ex-wife is setting you up now?" Sean asked with a chuckle.

Parker had already devoured half the pie. "Right? I was asking myself the same question. But apparently she's some ex-model from Connecticut that was referred to DNM."

"By whom? And what are we supposed to do with an ex-model?"

"Remember that guy Trent went into business with? What's his name? Desdune, I think."

Sean nodded. "Yeah, his family owns Lucien's, those Creole restaurants. They just opened a new one in Orlando. Great food."

"Right. Right. I remember them."

Of course Parker remembered good food, Sean almost said.

"Well, they married into this other family from Bennett Communications. She's the daughter, Adriana."

While Parker emptied his beer, Sean tried to piece together everything his cousin had just said. Jaydon was Parker's ex-wife. She ran Donovan Network Management, providing agents and talent scouts throughout the country. It still amazed Sean that his cousin, who was only a year older than he and two years younger than Dion, had been married and divorced before he'd turned thirty—a subject no one was allowed to talk about beyond the fact that the two remained friends and Jaydon still worked for them. Now, at thirty-two, Parker was a bachelor in great demand.

"I still don't get why Jaydon's setting you up on dates."

"I don't know, man. Women are crazy. She said something about maybe giving her a host job on the network. I don't know. I'm going to check her out tonight to see if she's got any potential."

Sean leaned back in the chair. "I guess that makes sense."

"Savian's asking when we're going to be ready to propose our idea for the magazine show. I think we're solid, but there's another part of the magazine we should include," Parker said, leaning over the island to pull a napkin from the stainless-steel holder.

"I know. Dion told me you were asking about our 'Ask Jenny' columnist."

Parker slammed a hand on the marble countertop. "Right. You know how many hits that column is getting online? More than any other page of the magazine. People seem desperate for the kind of help she's dishing out."

Sean nodded. He couldn't argue with the facts.

"I hope she's not some old chick, speaking from a

past of broken hearts. That's not going to be a good visual."

"She's not old," Sean said.

"Good. Is she married? That'll make her seem more stable, like she's achieved the dream."

He shook his head. "She's divorced. She has a kid though."

Parker looked like he was contemplating that fact. "We don't have to broadcast that."

"I just don't know," Sean said, even though he was not really sure what his objection to this idea was.

"Look, we've got to boost ratings. Reality shows are kicking butt all over the networks. We've got to jump in while the water's still clear."

"We can't build our name by imitating others," he said seriously. A part of the reason why the Donovan media conglomerate succeeded was by being innovative and attentive to detail. Rushing headlong into some trend could backfire on them."

"And we won't survive unless we're willing to change with the times." Parker held up his hand to stop whatever Sean was getting ready to say. "Just give it some thought. Read the column yourself and get a feel for what we can do. And I'd love to meet with the columnist, see if she's got some thoughts on the idea."

"I'll check it out," Sean said. It was his job to do just that, regardless of what a surprise Ms. Tate Dennison had been to him.

"Aren't you going to be late for your date?" he asked Parker when he noted his cousin was once again in his refrigerator.

With a chuckle, Parker took an apple. "I'm meeting her just down the street at the Four Seasons."

"You're heading to the Four Seasons for dinner and you're in here raiding my fridge like you're starving?"

Parker laughed.

"You always shop like you've got a house full of kids in here. It's either raid your fridge or drive all the way to the Big House to raid your mom's."

"What about your mom's fridge? Aunt Carol loves to cook," Sean said, as they once again made their way down the foyer toward the door.

Parker groaned. "She also loves to nag me about my past mistakes and when I'm going to fix everything by remarrying and having some kids."

With a nod, Sean conceded to knowing exactly what Parker meant. Not that his mother was nagging him to remarry. However, Janean was definitely in the market for grandchildren. Even though Dion was now married to Lyra, there was no talk of them having children yet. Which left the attention centered firmly on Sean.

"Then *mi casa es su casa*," Sean said with a smack on his cousin's back and a chuckle.

"Right. Call me tomorrow and we'll talk more about your columnist."

As Sean closed the door, he couldn't help but think of Tate Dennison as just that—his columnist. *His*. Shaking his head, he went back into the kitchen to find himself some dinner.

Chapter 4

She was fussing for nothing. He wouldn't come to her office twice in one week. That presumption was based on the fact that up until yesterday, he hadn't been to her office in the three months she'd worked there.

It didn't matter that she now thought her dress was too tight and too short. In the mirror behind her bedroom door it had looked perfectly fine. The black bolero jacket made the white-and-black printed dress look more professional. The wide yellow belt at her waist gave it a cheerful edge. On her feet were black sandals with three-and-a-half-inch heels and straps up to the ankle. They were office attire, just as her dress was, even though it only flirted against her kneecaps.

Her clothes weren't a big deal, she told herself again. She wasn't in the market for a man and most definitely not a Donovan. Not that she didn't think she deserved a good man, but Tate was just tired of the game. Boy meets girl. They go out and both try to impress each other with lies and posturing. They get married, and they have a huge, beautiful ceremony that they will likely be paying off for years after the wedding. Then come the babies and the monotony. Inevitably one would get tired of the other and the infidelities would begin. It was like one big circle that adults continuously ran through. But not her, not again.

Sean Donovan had come to her office for something yesterday, although he had never really said what. That meant he was liable to come back. She sighed, sinking into her chair. Her computer was already on, but she hadn't yet begun to work. The trip to the kitchenette where the coffee machines were had taken longer than she anticipated because her coworkers were very curious about her personal life as well as the personal life of every other employee in the office. It was damn tiring to stand there and listen to gossip she didn't give two cents about. But if she walked away she'd be deemed antisocial, and the work environment she was just beginning to get used to would turn sour.

Now she was going through her emails as steam circled around the top of her coffee mug that read "No. 1 Mom." She'd bought it for herself this past Mother's Day. If nobody else was going to appreciate her, she would have to do it for herself. Hey, hadn't she given that advice to a reader before? Probably, she thought with a smile.

Ten minutes into the emails, after she'd transferred a couple to the appropriate subfolders and deleted a few more, she came across one that made her catch her breath.

Need to speak with you about the column. Are you available today at 4:30?

No, was her immediate thought. Her mind screamed it over and over again. But her fingers—traitors that they were—had already begun typing her response.

Yes.

She hit Send and groaned. Evidently there was reason for her to worry about how the dress looked after all.

"If you sell me *Infinity,* I'll keep the name and you can keep your job," Sabine Ravenell said in her sultry voice.

Sean tried not to laugh at her and straightened his gray-and-latte Bulgari tie. He'd worn a suit the color of milk chocolate with shoes a darker shade of brown. At his wrists, gold cufflinks sparkled. Sean was a man of detail, whether in business or his personal appearance. He paid attention to everything and strived for the best, no matter what he did.

"I have no fear that my job's in jeopardy," he said simply. "*Infinity* is not for sale."

Sabine crossed her legs. She wore a purple skirt, short, as usual. Her purple jacket fit her bodice tightly but not in a bad way. She was definitely an attractive woman. With her light complexion and curly black hair that hung past her shoulders, she looked extremely beautiful and intoxicatingly sexy.

Nevertheless, Sean still wasn't interested. At all.

"Everything has a price," she told him.

"I think you mean every*one* has a price. In this case, that assumption would also be wrong."

Her elbows were propped on the arms of the chair. She tilted her head and touched a finger to her chin. It was a practiced pose, probably designed to hit a man right in the gut with a serious punch of lust. Sean felt a mild tapping of desire but squashed it.

"Look, there's no point in continuing with these discussions. The magazine is not for sale. And if it were, you'd be coming to the wrong man to make your deal."

She waved her other hand, the one still stroking a finger over her chin. "Dion's got his mind on other things," she said dismissively.

Sean knew exactly what she was getting at. More than one tabloid had reported the downfall of Dion Donovan because he'd gotten married. But Sean knew better—his brother's personality wasn't tied to the playboy image the press had painted on him. So the only thing marrying Lyra had done was make him extremely happy.

"Dion's mind is always here at *Infinity*. Don't let the marriage fool you."

Sabine threw her head back and laughed. Too hard and too loud, he thought.

"You Donovan boys are certainly a treat to do business with. Dion's content to let you handle the business with me. Why are you complaining? Not ready to live up to the Donovan name? Can't fill big brother's shoes?"

That finger had traced a line from her chin, down her neck to the cleavage she boldly displayed. When she licked her lips and raised an eyebrow suggestively, Sean wanted to laugh again. She was certainly pulling out all the stops with this meeting. Which in itself was laughable, since this was the third time he'd met with her to decline her offer to buy *Infinity*. He wondered how many more times it would take before she finally got the hint.

"I can assure you, Ms. Ravenell, I'm very confident in my position."

"And I'm very confident in mine," was her reply. "We need to come to a meeting of the minds. This offer is too good to pass up."

With that remark, she uncrossed her legs, leaving them open just enough so that—if he wanted to—he could see between her legs, but *that* was the last thing he wanted to get a glimpse of.

"The offer is too ludicrous to consider. Now, if you'll excuse me, I have another meeting."

He was already standing to escort her out of his office. Enough was enough. Her come-on had long since passed the line of mildly flattering to borderline disgusting. He'd be embarrassed for her if he thought she in some way deserved even that much from him. But Sean knew Sabine's game. He knew she played it well and with many. He wasn't about to become her next victim, no matter how hard she tried.

"Think about it, Sean. Who knows, maybe I'll even make you my partner. You'd have Dion's job and more money and power than you know what to do with," she told him as she stood, flipping her hair over her shoulder with another one of her practiced moves.

"I have a job. I have money. And power is overrated. The door's that way," he told her with a nod of his head.

He wasn't even going to walk her out. She'd taken up enough of his time as it was with chatter that didn't interest him one bit.

Besides, it was almost four-twenty-five. He'd asked Tate to meet him here at four-thirty. On his desk were her last three columns, two of which had received more than eighty thousand hits on the website. He didn't have any more time to spare Sabine or her crazy offer.

When he was alone again he picked up a piece of paper and began to read. The title was "Stuck on Stupid." He read the article, shaking his head at the man who took his girlfriend back even after she'd cheated on him with her ex-boyfriend…twice. She stole money from him, stole his credit cards and ran up the balances, and still, when she came knocking on his door again, crying that she loved him, he took her back.

Sean's first impulse was to concede. "You are stuck on stupid, buddy."

Tate's answer was a little more diplomatic.

Dear SOS,
Being in love can sometimes be construed as being stupid, but that's a misconception. I'm quoting the Bible here: "Love is patient. Love is kind." Love is not selfish or hurtful or devious. Your girlfriend is all of the above. So my solution for you is that for just a few minutes out of your life, you'll have to adopt some of those same traits. You'll have to selfishly claim your feelings as being more important than hers. Then you'll probably hurt her feelings when you tell her to leave. Devious is what she may call you when you file charges against her for stealing your credit cards. This may not come as easily to you as it obviously does to her, but it's necessary.

He stopped reading when a knock sounded at his door. Leaving the papers on his desk, Sean stood. He straightened his tie and did a quick breath check before crossing the room to answer the door.

"Hello," he said when she looked up at him.

"Hi," she replied with a smile that totally took his breath away.

"Ah, come on in." He cleared his throat after a few stalled seconds. "Have a seat."

Closing the door, Sean watched her walk to the guest chair across from his desk. It was wrong, or at least it should have been, the way he watched the sway of her bottom in the fitted dress. Yesterday her dress had been more full and she'd been leaning over, so he couldn't really get a good look at her body. Not that he had been trying to.

But today, this dress left no doubt in his mind that she was a very attractive woman. The heels she wore made her toned calves look almost succulent, while the bright belt at her waist gave her an hourglass shape. He needed to get behind his desk before making any further assessments or risk the possibility of a sexual harassment suit when she looked up and his thoughts were clearly betrayed through his growing erection.

She started talking the minute he sat down. "I'm not sure what this is about. I haven't missed a deadline, have I?"

"No. Nothing like that," he began, shaking his head as he gathered up the papers, stacking them neatly. "I've been reading some of your columns."

She sat up straight and he noticed that he couldn't see up her skirt, unlike with Sabine. Her hands were folded in her lap and she looked at him quizzically with those eyes. Deep brown eyes that made him want to ask how her day was, what she'd had for lunch, what she planned to have for dinner.

Sean cleared his throat once more and tried to re-route his thoughts. "You're very insightful and tend to hit the mark with stunning accuracy without being too preachy. There's a good tone to the column. I really like that," he told her. "We really like that. And by 'we,' I mean upper management."

She nodded as if following the conversation but still waiting for the other shoe to drop. Her hair hung just past her shoulders, straight as an arrow and black as night, with honey-brown highlights. Yesterday, he remembered, it had a little curl to it. He blinked to keep from staring.

"As you know, we're an affiliate of Donovan Network Television."

Her head moved in another nod. Her hands didn't move, weren't shaking nervously, just sat perfectly still. She was patient; she'd waited for things before and was used to it, he surmised. Then he figured he'd just blurt it out, since the thought of making this woman wait wasn't very appealing to him.

"We're thinking of possibly adding a slot to an entertainment program that's still in development. The slot would consist of you giving your relationship advice on air."

Tate wanted to gasp. She wanted to ask him if he was serious or if he was sure he had the right person. Instead she cleared her throat and sat up even straighter. "You want the 'Ask Jenny' column to go live?" she asked, as panic and excitement fought for a prominent position inside her stomach.

"We think it would go over well. How would you feel about that?"

"What would be the format?" she asked over the lump in her throat. This was definitely not what she'd expected when she came to his office. Not at all.

"I don't know. We haven't really gotten that far in the planning. I wanted to see how you'd feel about doing a television show. I mean, obviously that's not the job you applied for."

"Obviously," she said, then she smiled because she didn't want him to think she was being sarcastic. "I mean, I have a degree in journalism, so I don't know much about television."

"So you like writing the column?"

She nodded. "I do. I've always loved writing."

He sat back, watching her closely. Too closely for Tate's comfort. But she wouldn't show how nervous she was. She couldn't afford to. It was her firm belief that once a man knew your weakness he'd exploit it, and you. As for Tate, she'd been there and done that.

"Do you enjoy giving advice to the lovelorn?"

It was a simple question. She shouldn't have felt like he was really asking her something deeper, more personal. Yet, the way his calm, assessing eyes held her gaze, she couldn't help but feel a little exposed.

"I like giving new insight into situations. Sometimes when you're the one involved, you can't see the truth or realize other alternatives to help you react to the truth. That's what my advice provides, an alternative to the relationship they're currently involved in."

"But you believe in love?" he asked, still sitting back in his chair, his fingers rubbing over his goatee.

"I mean, you've been in love before, so you've had some experience in the area?"

"Yes," Tate answered, a little less enthusiastically than she'd been speaking before. "I have been in love." Then, because she knew this line of questioning might be just a bit out of context, judging by the way he was still looking at her, she asked him, "Have you ever been in love, Mr. Donovan?"

Chapter 5

He was only minutely surprised by her question. Candor came easily to this woman. She was polished and intelligent and confident, all traits he admired in a woman.

The fact that she was extremely attractive hadn't escaped him either. Before he'd known it, his questions had taken a personal edge, and his interest in her had gone just beyond what might be appropriate.

"I have never been in love with a woman," he told her and wondered what it was about her that made it so easy to be honest.

She nodded as if that was the answer she'd expected. "It's an adventure, I'll tell you that," she said lightly.

Her eyes said something totally different. The deep depths said it was also painful. Whoever she'd been in love with had hurt her, badly. That thought made Sean angry.

"Would you like to have dinner with me?" he asked. Her eyes widened as if she thought the question was sudden or surprising. Sean didn't think it was either. Whatever he did or said came after much thought on his part. He'd been thinking about this woman since first seeing her yesterday afternoon. For Sean, that meant something.

"Ah, no," she began after a few seconds of blinking and staring at him in awe. "I don't think that would be appropriate, considering we work together."

He smiled. "You're not going to get into trouble. I'm the boss, remember?"

Her smile came easily, and deep dimples in both her cheeks twinkled at him. "That's precisely why I said dinner would be inappropriate."

He could do nothing but nod. Her response was logical and most likely one he would have used himself if a female at the office had come on to him. But this was different. He didn't know why specifically, he just knew that it was.

She was looking at her watch when he thought to say something else in response, so he said instead, "Am I keeping you from another engagement? Another dinner date perhaps?"

It hadn't been established whether she was involved with someone. He wanted to know the answer, but then again he didn't.

"I need to pick my daughter up from day care," was her reply.

Her daughter, right. He'd forgotten she had a child. "Then let's go," he said, standing from his desk and retrieving his suit jacket from the back of his chair. "I'll walk you to your car."

She looked as if she were going to argue, then she stopped with a shrug and left the office.

The parking garage was accessed by taking an elevator to the lobby floor of the building and using an enclosed walkway. Tate always parked on the highest floor, afraid that the lower ones weren't as protected from theft. Sean rode the elevator up to level four with her in silence, silence for which she was grateful.

There was so much going through her mind at the moment. His offer of a television show, his interest in her work, and, of course, him asking her out to dinner. Where had that come from? She had no clue. Before yesterday, she'd never seen this man in person. She'd heard of him and his family, of course, but she would have never guessed he'd heard of her in any capacity. Yes, her immediate supervisor seemed pleased with her work, and she'd assumed the growing number of letters signaled she was doing a good job. But she could never have imagined anything to the extent of this type of promotion. *Get a grip,* she told herself. Her life was a perfect example of how all good things did not necessarily have a positive outcome.

"My car's this way," she said when they stepped off the elevator.

Her voice echoed in the enclosed space, and she quickly closed her mouth. On the cement floor her heels clicked. Beside her Sean held what she thought were his own car keys. His brown suit hung over long, muscled limbs, and an intoxicating manly cologne tickled her nostrils. A better-looking specimen she had yet to see up close and personal, and a small part of her treasured the moment—even if it was a totally professional one.

"Nice car," Sean said as they approached her midnight-blue Volvo.

She almost said she'd won it in the divorce settlement but figured that little tidbit of information was better kept a secret. "I like reliability," she said.

He nodded. "I can relate to that. Where does your daughter go to day care?"

Retrieving her own set of keys, Tate initiated the automatic door locks and reached for the handle. "Little Darlings Day Care. It's on Biscayne."

She leaned into the car to place her purse and bag inside when she glimpsed the passenger-side window. "Damn it!" she cursed before remembering she wasn't alone. Then on impulse she tried to right herself and banged her head on the interior roof of the car.

"Are you all right?" she could hear Sean asking from behind as his hands went to her hips.

She backed out of the car with Sean's assistance. Her hand went to her now throbbing head. "Sorry. Yes, I'm fine. But my window is broken."

"What window?"

She used her thumb to point toward the other side of her car as she started walking in that direction. Sean followed her and was once more privy to her cursing when she noted the back passenger window was also broken.

"Great. Just great," she said, stepping on shattered glass.

Sean had pulled his cell phone from his pocket and was already talking to someone. Tate was lifting a hand to the door handle when she felt his strong fingers at her wrist.

"Don't touch anything else. If it was a break-in, the police will need to dust for prints," he told her.

"A break-in. Right," she said. With a clutch in her chest, she leaned forward to look through the broken window.

Her gasp made Sean move in closer. "What's wrong?"

With a hand to her throat, Tate said, "Briana's car seat is gone. Who would break into a car to steal a baby's car seat?"

"Come on," Sean said, moving her away from the car. "Let's stand over here and wait for the police."

The police arrived in minutes and did what they called "processing the scene." They took pictures and did something that would lift prints. Questions were fired at her left and right. "What's missing?" "What time do you get to work?" "Do you get here the same time every day?" "Park in the same spot?" On and on and on it went until she·wanted to scream.

She still needed to pick up Briana, and now her only mode of transportation was being detained. Sean insisted on having the windows fixed, and since she didn't have the extra five hundred dollars—which was her insurance deductible—Tate didn't refuse his offer. It was when he offered to take her to get Briana that she tensed a bit more.

"That's not necessary. I can take a cab," she told him.

He was already shaking his head. "You're not taking a cab all the way down to Biscayne and then back to your house," he said adamantly. "I'm having the car towed the minute the cops are finished. The windows should be fixed by tomorrow afternoon."

"It's not a big deal. I can take a cab tonight and then again in the morning to get to work," she said, afraid to calculate the cost of doing both. *Infinity* paid her a decent salary for a writer, but that salary had to stretch to cover rent on her apartment and all the expenses that entailed, as well as day care and food for her and Briana. She wasn't completely destitute, but there wasn't a whole lot of breathing room within her budget. Still, the thought of her boss going out of his way like that just didn't feel right to her.

"You're not taking a cab, and that's final," he said in a tone that was supposed to emphasize his words.

It did, to an extent. Tate figured it was rude to continue to turn down his generosity, and that surely wouldn't bode well as far as her new promotion. So she let the officers get her purse and bag out of the car as she stood across the garage waiting. When they were done and the tow truck had arrived, Sean gave the driver his business card and told him to have the autoglass shop call him first thing tomorrow morning. She didn't bristle too much—after all, the garage was a part of the building owned by the Donovans. If her car was vandalized on their property, he might feel responsible.

But when he ushered her to his metallic Mercedes CLS63 coupe, she sucked in a breath.

"What's wrong? You don't like my car?" he asked with a half smile that made her insides quiver.

She was shaking her head as he opened the passenger door and motioned for her to get in. "That's not it," she said, sliding into the leather seat. "I'm just trying to figure out how Briana's going to sit in a backseat that's not much bigger than her."

So his car wasn't equipped for a baby, Sean thought as he drove through rush-hour traffic downtown. That's because he was a single man with no children. Still, that didn't stop him from looking through his rearview mirror to the small backseat of the car every few minutes.

Tate hadn't said another word after getting in and buckling her seatbelt. She wasn't happy with the developments, he could tell. But there was no way around this. He wasn't about to let her get a cab to the day care and then to her house. Despite the cost, he just wouldn't have been able to sleep tonight knowing he'd watched her do such a thing. Especially since he had no other plans for tonight. There was no reason why he couldn't take the time to pick up her daughter and drive them home. It was a simple act of kindness, he told himself repeatedly.

"You can pull in right here. I'll just run in and get her," Tate said when the yellow-and-white building became visible.

Sean did as she told him and pulled up close to the curb. "Do you need any help?" he asked.

She smiled before getting out. "No. I can handle this part on my own."

He nodded, figuring she did this every day. For him, being at a day-care center was a totally different experience. Curious, he watched other parents coming out with toddlers in hand. Two mothers came out of the double swinging doors, one with a little boy who held on to his bottle, tipping his little head back to drink as he walked. The other woman had a daughter with her, a cute little girl with ribbons in her hair and a pink jacket. They would go home and have dinner…and then what? he wondered.

Minutes later Tate came through that very same door. Sean watched with a touch more curiosity than he had with the others. She held her baby in her arms and had a small pink backpack with bright green polka dots in her hand. The baby was the same pretty caramel complexion as Tate, with plump cheeks and smiling eyes that he could see more clearly as she came closer to the car.

Sean immediately got out and jogged around to the passenger side door. "We should have stopped by the store to get a car seat," he said, opening the door for her once more.

"It's okay, I have an extra one at home that I received as a baby shower gift. But for now the school has one they're going to let me borrow. Could you just push this seat up so they can install it?"

"Sure," he said as he pushed the seat upward. When he turned back around, there was an older woman with wire-rimmed glasses standing behind him, holding a car seat almost as big as she was.

"I'll get that," he told her. He was rewarded with a quick thank-you and smile, instead of the argument he probably would have received had Tate been the one holding the seat.

She wasn't like other women he met who were accepting, and sometimes even demanding, when he offered them help. No, she seemed to challenge him at every turn. Sean, being the problem solver that he was, couldn't help but wonder why.

The seat wasn't as easy to install as he would have liked. Tate was right—his backseat was too small for a child's car seat. Still, he got it positioned and buckled it in. When Tate leaned over to put her daughter into the seat, they both looked at the finished result.

"Her feet are cramped," Sean said, seeing her tiny

white shoes with pink-and-white laces slap immediately against the back of the seat.

"I'll pull my seat up and she'll be fine. My apartment's only about ten minutes from here," Tate said. "Thank you so much for doing this."

Her words were probably the only thing that could have drawn his attention away from the baby, who looked so much like her mother, especially when she smiled and dimples creased her chubby little cheeks.

"You don't have to thank me," he said sincerely. "We can swing by the store and purchase a new seat before I take you home."

She was shaking her head before he could finish his sentence.

"I already have another seat."

"But that's your backup," he heard himself saying as he went around to the driver side. She did say she had another seat; he should just let it go. But Sean knew he wouldn't.

By the time he climbed back into the car and began driving, Tate was again telling him she didn't need a car seat. Sean nodded, seemingly agreeing with her. But first thing tomorrow morning he knew he'd be in the store buying a car seat and a purple bunny to match the one on the pacifier Briana had in her mouth.

Chapter 6

"I don't want to sound redundant, but thank you," Tate said when they were in her apartment and Briana was happily playing in her playpen.

Sean held up a hand. "Don't worry about it. I'll send a car to pick you up tomorrow. What time do you need it to be here?"

"No, that's not necessary."

"Really, Tate. We seem to waste a lot of time with me making offers and you declining them. Now, you need to be at work tomorrow, especially since I'm going to try and arrange a meeting with Dion and Parker so we can go over ideas for your segment. And Briana needs to get safely to day care. So this is the best solution."

His calm tone was what did it. Patrick used to argue with her like they were siblings or even bitter enemies. Tate remembered the first time she'd questioned his all-night business meetings. That argument had gotten so loud it had awakened Briana and almost had the neighbors calling the cops on them.

But Sean was calm, and his eyes were warm as they looked down at her. His voice was compassionate yet stern. He was not expecting an argument. And Tate decided, reluctantly, that she wasn't going to give him one. "I appreciate that offer, Mr. Donovan."

His smile was quick and potent to the point where she completely lost her breath.

"Call me Sean."

Call her a doctor, because she was going to faint. Was he this sexy in the office? She wasn't sure. But standing in her small living room, he looked like some kind of contemporary god in a designer suit. His bald head made him look intriguing, and the neatly trimmed goatee that framed his firm lips had her heart hammering in her chest.

"She seems like a very happy child," he commented.

His voice interrupted thoughts that she shouldn't have been having in the first place, and Tate had to clear her throat to get herself together. "Ah, yes. She is very happy. She's everything to me."

He nodded and walked to stand close to the playpen. Slipping his hands into his pockets, Tate watched as his jacket was pushed back, his muscled chest revealed slightly. But it wasn't just the physical good looks he had. No, there was something else about this man that made him alluring.

"Where's her father?"

Like a splash of cold water, his words settled over her, and Tate instantly tensed.

"He's gone," was all she said. "I should really get her

dinner ready. We're already behind with our nightly schedule."

He didn't turn away from her but bent down so that now he was even closer to Briana. Tate took a protective step closer.

"She likes to play," he said when Briana had pulled herself up and was handing one of the many toys and rattles inside the playpen to Sean.

He took it and smiled down at her. Briana giggled and Tate felt something shifting inside her that she wasn't happy with.

"Sean, at the risk of sounding rude," she said, then she stopped when he turned to look up at her.

"Oh, no. You're right. You have things to do." He jiggled the rattle then returned it to Briana's chubby grasp. His smile spread as he continued to look at her daughter.

"I really appreciate everything you've done. If there's any way I can repay you for your generosity, just let me know. And if you could have the car here at seven, that will work just fine," she said, heading to the door and opening it for him.

Sean stood and walked to the door, where she was now standing. For a few moments he simply looked at her. Then he nodded. "Don't worry about it. I'll see you at the office. I'll give you a call if I'm able to arrange a meeting."

Tate nodded. "That's fine."

He was already through the door when he turned back to her. "On second thought, there is something you can do to repay me."

Tate almost sighed. She should have known it was too good to be true. All men wanted something eventually.

"What's that?"

"Have dinner with me tomorrow night. And before you say it, I'll take care of the babysitter issue."

She opened her mouth to say something, but he reached out and pushed her chin up until her mouth closed.

"See you in the morning, Tate."

"You need a what?" Regan uncrossed her long legs and leaned forward in the guest chair in Sean's office the next morning.

"A babysitter. I need one of you to babysit for me," he repeated himself even though he knew damned well she'd heard him the first time. Both of them had, but Lyra was staring at him quizzically as well. They were acting as if he'd spoken a foreign language.

"Just exactly who do you need a babysitter for?" Lyra asked next. Her voice was measurably lower than Regan's, as her personality wasn't as boisterous as his cousin's.

He'd called them both to his office after he'd arrived, an hour late. It had taken him much longer than he'd anticipated to find a baby store and then to decide on which model car seat to purchase—despite Tate's insistence that it wasn't necessary. He'd had a courier pick the seat up about twenty minutes ago and take it to the garage where her car windows were being repaired. When she picked up Briana after work she'd have a brand new car seat and Briana would have a new stuffed animal. Sean wasn't sure how pleased she'd be at his sneakiness, but he was feeling pretty damned good about it himself.

"I'm taking a woman out to dinner, and she'll need

a babysitter for her daughter," he said quickly, so as not to give either of them time to interrupt.

As it was, both of them only stared at him. Regan began rubbing a finger over her chin, her slanted eyes becoming mere slits. Lyra had leaned forward, and two silver bangles slid down her slim arm as she lifted them and propped her chin on her fists.

"What? You're looking at me like I'm some stranger," he said when the staring thing was becoming beyond odd.

"We're trying to figure out who you are and what you've done to the Sean we know and love," Lyra said.

Regan shook her head, and hoop earrings the size of his hand smacked her cheeks. "No. I'm wondering who this woman is who has a child and can't find her own babysitter."

"She's the staff writer who does the 'Ask Jenny' column. And the reason she's not getting her own babysitter is because I told her I'd take care of it."

"You, who does not have any children, will take care of finding a babysitter?" Regan asked. "And just how did you expect to do that?"

Lyra chuckled. "By calling us."

Sean nodded to his sister-in-law and smiled. "Now, which one of you would like to help me out?"

"That depends," Lyra said, sitting back in the chair and crossing her legs. "Is this a business dinner or a personal one?"

He'd known that was coming and was prepared to deal with it appropriately. "I want to talk to her about doing the television spot. I think my presentation will go over a lot better if we're in a more comfortable setting." He prayed they didn't see through the lie. It wasn't often that he lied to women, and lying to his family was even less frequent.

"You know there are babysitting services," Regan offered.

"I don't have time to research them and do background checks. Look, can I count on either one of you to help? Think of it as doing a favor for the company," he implored.

He could have called his cousin, Trent Donovan, who was an ex–Navy SEAL and now owned his own private investigation agency, which did quick background checks. But that's not what he wanted for Briana, not tonight. Sean wasn't sure why it was so important that a member of his family keep her. He'd worry about that later.

Lyra gave Regan a knowing look. "We'll both do it. What time?" she asked

"What?" Regan asked, turning to Lyra, who only continued to nod her head. Then, as if Regan finally caught on, she said, "Yeah, we'll do it."

"Great," was Sean's reply, even though he knew there was something behind their looks that he probably wasn't going to like. Again, he'd deal with that later. "We'll bring her to you at the Big House around seven," he told them, making up the plans as he went.

His temples throbbed a bit at the impulsivity of this entire situation, but his heart hammered with the beginnings of excitement. When was the last time he'd felt this way about something that wasn't totally business? He couldn't remember. What he did know for a fact was that tonight's dinner with Tate Dennison wasn't all about *Infinity,* not by a long shot.

* * *

She'd agreed to go out with the boss. All day long, Tate had been thinking of what she'd gotten herself into. Or actually, what the person who'd tried to break into her car had gotten her into. Were it not for the shattered windows on her car and the missing car seat she wouldn't be indebted to Sean and left with no other option but to go out with him tonight.

She didn't want to go on a date with Sean Donovan.

If she spoke that aloud someone would think she was crazy. Especially Ashton, the receptionist on this floor, who thought the sun and moon both took their cues from the Donovan men that ran this magazine.

"Girl, I'd take either one of them any day of the week. Okay, well not Dion, since he's already spoken for, and I actually like Lyra. But Sean and Parker are still fair game," she'd told Tate one day at lunch.

Tate hadn't really been interested in the conversation. She'd resolved not to dream or even hope about another involvement with a man—even if it was a Donovan. Ashton, on the other hand, couldn't think of anything else.

"What about Savian?" she'd asked, just because he was the only Donovan man that frequented the magazine that wasn't married and that Ashton hadn't already mentioned.

She'd scrunched her face a little and Tate almost laughed. "He's a little on the uptight side. But, you know what, he's still fine, so I'd give him a try, too."

They'd laughed about that and much of the other gossip Ashton had fed her that day. Gossip that Tate was glad her name had not been connected to—although that could have been a convenient deletion on Ashton's part.

Tate knew Ashton wasn't the only female who worked at the magazine who felt that way about this particular family of men. Hell, the family stretched all the way to the West Coast. That meant that most likely there were thousands of other women who felt the same way. And if this had been four years ago and she didn't know what she knew now about relationships, Tate might have had those same stars in her eyes.

But it wasn't. And she didn't. At least she was going to convince herself that she didn't.

In front of her office building she met O'Shea, the rotund Caucasian man with the balding head and cheerful laugh, who'd picked her and Briana up this morning. He was driving a town car, long and shining, almost like a limousine.

"Afternoon to ya, ma'am," he spoke with an Irish accent that matched his piercing blue eyes. She was willing to bet that before his hair had turned snowy white and taken a permanent leave of absence it had been carrot-colored.

"Good afternoon," she said, heading toward the back passenger door. She slipped inside and put her purse and bag on the seat next to her, and then did a double take.

"Where's Briana's car seat?" she asked as soon as O'Shea climbed into the front seat.

"Oh, took that back to your apartment just like Mr. Donovan told me to."

"But how's she going to get home?"

"He said to take you to the repair shop. That's what I'm gonna do."

O'Shea put the car in Drive, humming a tune to himself as Tate stared out the window, hating that she'd have to borrow the day care's car seat again.

"How was your day?" O'Shea asked when it seemed he'd grown tired of humming the song.

"Great," she murmured. "Just great." Not very interested in idle chit-chat, she looked out the window, watching the city pass them by.

"Young, pretty woman like you should always have a great day," he said, peeking at her through the rearview mirror.

"That's not always how it goes," was her bland reply.

"Do not work too hard," he told her. "Take time to— what do you say…ah—smell the blossoms."

His round head was nodding up and down with so much force his jaws shook. Tate couldn't help but smile. He looked like the jovial grandfather little girls loved to visit. Which made her feel a pang of homesickness. Her mother had died when she was thirteen. She was raised by her father and grandfather, who were still alive and kicking, as far as she knew. They lived in a big old house on Maryland's Eastern Shore. If she closed her eyes she could still see the porch with the weather-beaten siding and the front door with the lock that would grab hold of a key for dear life, coughing it out and releasing the latch only after a good fight. With a sigh, she sat back against the seat.

"Well, when someone shows me the blossoms in my life, I'll take time to sniff them," she said and felt a wave of pity that almost choked her.

Tate hated that feeling, hated feeling sorry for herself when she knew that ultimately she'd done what she thought was right. Everyone made mistakes, that's what her mother used to tell her. It was what they learned from the mistakes that mattered. So what had she learned: not to trust another man with her heart ever again.

Pulling into the garage, she decided O'Shea didn't really qualify as a man she shouldn't trust, so she gave him a huge smile and thank-you for his services. It was when she went to tip him that he frowned.

"No. No. Keep your money. I just do my job," he told her.

"But I want to. You've been so nice to me and my daughter today. Let me repay you. It's not much," she insisted.

They stood amid cars in various stages of disrepair. Behind them was a building about a half a block long, and through the open archways she could see cars up on the lift with mechanics standing beneath them reaching into the insides. It was a sunny day with a slight breeze that ruffled the ends of Tate's ponytail.

O'Shea reached for the hand she held the forty dollars in, then he grasped her other wrist and held them both together. "Keep your money. You work for it. Buy a pretty dress and go out on the town. Have some fun," he said, his eyes alight with what he thought was a fabulous idea.

She opened her mouth, almost telling him she had a date tonight, but she refrained. It was not a date. It was a thank-you dinner, and that's all, she assured herself.

"Thank you," she told O'Shea, not willing to insult him by insisting he take her money.

"Now, go get your car. I'll wait to see that everything is okay."

With a nod she went to a small office where she assumed the manager would be.

"Hello," she said, knocking on the window.

There were two people sitting behind desks. One male and a female who was chewing gum as if it tasted like filet mignon.

"Hello, I'm here to pick up my car. I'm Tate Dennison," she yelled through the Plexiglas when neither of them seemed quick to greet her.

They looked perplexed, and she figured out what the issue was. "Mr. Donovan sent my car here to be fixed. The back passenger-side window."

The man was up and out of the office so fast Tate almost thought he was rushing to use the bathroom instead of coming to see her. A few seconds later he stood in front of her.

"Sure. Sure. The Volvo. It's all done, ma'am," he told her. "I'll be right back."

A few minutes later her car pulled up in front of her. Tate took the keys happily and slipped behind the driver's seat. It was a good feeling to be in her own car, about to go pick up her daughter. She wasn't used to being driven around or catered to in any way. The car was already running and she was about to shift into gear when she heard a horn beep. It was O'Shea, already in his car. She waved and smiled at him and drove out of the parking lot.

Tate glanced at her watch and wondered if she had time to circle back to her apartment and get the car seat. She quickly looked in the rearview mirror and gasped. There was a car seat already there, and it wasn't hers. Sean Donovan had gone overboard. She figured she really did have to attend this dinner after all.

Chapter 7

Tate's doorbell rang at precisely ten minutes to seven. She'd arrived home after picking up Briana at five-forty-five. After a quick wash-up and a meal of chicken, rice and barely consumed green beans, Briana had fallen asleep while playing in her playpen. Tate used that opportunity to grab a quick shower and toss three dresses on to the bed. She'd stared at them for about ten minutes and then closed her eyes and pointed.

The cobalt-blue dress won. Slipping it on, she was thankful for Weight Watchers Online, which got her back to her regular size 12. She still had a bit of a paunch around the waist and stretch marks that could go on for days in that same area, but that was fine. The dress was fitted across her breasts with a soft, flowing material that flared out from her bodice down to the middle of her thigh. She'd just slipped on pewter sandals with four-inch heels that would surely make her legs look more svelte than thick, as they'd been called in the past by her sister. She clasped her earrings on after she slid on a three-inch-wide bangle, then jumped when the doorbell rang.

She placed a palm to her stomach and attempted to steady her breathing as she stared at herself in the mirror. The steam from the shower had curled her hair, and she'd decided not to fuss with it. Instead she'd opted for a thin silver headband and fluffed the curls until they fell in big, happy ringlets over her shoulders.

"It's just dinner," she told herself. She'd been saying that for the last hour, volleying back and forth with, "I'm not going."

Considering the fact that behind her front door was no doubt Sean Donovan, she'd say the "It's just dinner" side had won. When the bell sounded again, Tate left her bedroom and went to answer it.

"I was starting to think I'd been stood up," he said with a smile that washed over her like that warm shower she'd just taken.

Tate plastered her own nervous smile on and tried to breathe normally. "No. I was just getting some last-minute things together for Briana."

"Oh, I love babies. Can I see her?" the woman to Sean's right asked.

Her presence came as a surprise, and it almost rendered Tate speechless. There were two women with him.

"Ah, sure. Come in," she said, taking a step back.

"Tate Dennison, this is my sister-in-law, Lyra Donovan. And this is my cousin, Regan."

She swallowed and then spoke to the two attractive women standing in front of her. "It's nice to meet you."

Lyra approached her first. A petite woman with a quiet style, she immediately extended her hand and a warm smile to Tate.

"It's a pleasure. I love your column," Lyra said.

Regan stepped up next, shaking Tate's hand. "I've been reading the column as well. I'm learning a lot from your candid advice. Great job," Regan said.

"Thank you. You do a great job with the fashion piece as well," was Tate's reply.

Regan smiled, and Tate thought she'd never seen a prettier woman. Her slanted eyes lifted slightly, golden brown skin sparkled beneath impeccable makeup and her hair was perfectly styled in soft, feathery waves framing her face.

"A woman after my own heart. Fashion is *numero uno*." Regan grinned at Tate.

"And here's the baby." Lyra sighed, looking down into the playpen, where Briana lay still asleep. "She's precious."

Regan crossed the room to stand beside Lyra. "A diva in the making. Just look how she owns this little bed, like she dares anyone to try and take her place."

The women chuckled and Sean took a step closer to Tate. "I hired them to babysit Briana while we have dinner. Is that okay with you?"

Like she was really going to stand here and say no.

"It's fine, if they're okay with it." She looked over at the playpen nervously to see the two women still peering down at her daughter. "Have they ever taken care of a baby?" she asked, trying to lower her voice a bit.

Regan didn't look like she'd taken care of anyone

but herself, and Tate was a little concerned with her long manicured nails and how she would handle Briana. Lyra looked like she possibly had some nurturing instincts. In fact, the woman looked as if she were dying to pick Briana up.

"I think so," was Sean's answer. "But they're going to take her to my mother's house, so Briana will be in the best hands once she gets there."

"What? To your mother's? Why?" That was not good. Tate's stomach plummeted at that thought. This was just going too far. "She can't go to your mother's."

He looked perplexed at her words. "Why? Is something wrong with my mother's house?"

She immediately shook her head. "No. That's not what I'm saying. It's just that," Tate paused and took a deep breath. "This is just a business dinner, Sean. It's not like it's a real date. Involving your family is a little bit much for me." She told him honestly.

Briana whimpered and she stepped past Sean to see that Lyra had finally given in and bent down to pick her up. "Awww, she smells so sweet. Just like a baby." The rest of the sentences were a series of coos and gurgles that solicited a sleepy-eyed grin from Briana.

The next thing to grab Tate's attention was a hand to her elbow. A hand that sent sparks of heat spearing through her body.

"She'll be okay, Tate. I promise they won't let anything happen to her. You're allowed to have some adult time."

Adult time? What was that? Besides when she was at work, there wasn't a moment since Briana's birth that Tate was not with her. After Patrick left, she couldn't even stomach the thought. That probably meant she centered too much time and attention on her only child, but Tate wasn't in the mood to analyze herself right now. Briana was her responsibility and nobody else's, and that was that.

"Look," she said, turning so that she could slip her arm from his grasp. "This might not be such a good idea."

"It's a fantastic idea," Regan said, coming up from behind. "You go out and let Sean buy you a fabulously expensive dinner and some kickass wine, and then you can come past the Big House and pick up Briana. Aunt Janean is going to love having a baby in the house again. And this way you and Sean can talk about your column becoming a part of the magazine show."

As she'd talked, Regan had been pushing Tate toward the door, thrusting her purse in her hand as they passed the end table.

"Lyra's got all her things, right?" Regan asked.

Lyra nodded her head as she slipped the already packed baby bag onto one shoulder, holding a now smiling and clapping Briana against her hip. "We're all set."

"The car seat," Tate said. "You can use that one since there's a new one in my car." Her gaze fell to Sean, who simply shrugged.

"Just call me the fairy godfather," he said, moving to open the door.

"I don't believe in fairy tales," Tate said, glancing at him as she walked past.

Tate meant every word of what she'd said. She didn't believe in fairy tales—at least not anymore. But even she had to admit that her date with Sean had taken on a quietly romantic feel.

She sat in the passenger seat of his sleek car and watched as they pulled up in front of the Capitol Grill. After handing his keys to the valet, Sean went around to her side of the car and offered her his arm. She'd taken it, because...what else was she going to do?

As they entered the restaurant and the maître d' greeted them with all smiles and unflagging manners, Tate felt the first moments of privilege. She was with a Donovan; she shouldn't expect anything less. Yet the feeling was a little uncomfortable, since she'd never experienced it before.

They were led to a table in the center of a room, and she noted that there were several tables around the one where they were being seated, but none of them were occupied.

The restaurant was gorgeous with its Old World, elegant feel. It was all dark cherrywoods, deep cranberry Aubusson carpet, tables covered with impeccably pressed white linens and sparkling crystal glasses. In the center, a small ivory lamp glowed with entrancing life.

So much for this being just a casual dinner.

"Relax," Sean said, pulling her attention away from the decor and the fact that she just might be in over her head.

"I'm fine," she lied.

He was about to say something when the waiter returned to switch their white linen napkins with black ones to avoid any lint getting on their clothes. "Can I get you something to drink? Something from your private stock, Mr. Donovan?"

Sean nodded. "We're sort of celebrating tonight, so

yes, bring a bottle of Dom, the Rosé. Put it on ice and bring two glasses of water to start."

"Excellent, sir."

"You're not fine," Sean said, picking up the conversation where they'd been interrupted.

She opened her napkin, placed it in her lap and squared her shoulders. "What do you think we're celebrating?" she asked, attempting to change the subject.

He looked at her like he knew exactly what she was doing but only shrugged. "Parker's really convinced that the relationship segment should be added to the show. I have to agree with him. So we're celebrating your rise from staff writer to relationship expert."

She sighed. "Please, I am definitely no expert in that arena."

"Really? You seem to be on point with all your responses to the letters. I'd think you had experiences that taught you a lot."

"Taught me what *not* to do," she said with a frown. Their water was delivered and she lifted her glass for a drink.

"Ready to order?" the waiter asked with a smile.

He didn't wait on any of the other patrons in the restaurant, Tate was sure. He smiled at her as if he'd gotten dressed today and come in just to see her. She was flattered and decided to relax and enjoy the preferential treatment. Who knew when she'd receive it again?

"Let's start with the pan-fried calamari and hot cherry peppers," Sean said, not even looking at his menu. "Is spicy all right with you?"

His voice had lowered a bit when he asked that question, and Tate fumbled with her menu as she looked up at him. "That's fine." Mentally she told herself not to say "fine" again for the duration of the night.

She ordered lobster and crab-stuffed shrimp, while Sean went with the chef's selection of Kona-crusted dry-aged sirloin with caramelized shallot butter.

"What happened with you and Briana's father?"

Tate almost choked on her second glass of water. Clearing her throat and using her napkin to wipe her lips, she said, "You don't beat around the bush do you?"

"Never saw the need to," he stated flatly. "If you want to know the answer to a question, then ask the question."

"So I can ask you anything I want and you'll answer me?"

"Sure. There's no reason for me not to."

She contemplated that for a minute.

"You like changing the subject," Sean said, "But I don't confuse easily. What happened with you and Briana's father?"

Tate couldn't help but admire his persistence. A man shouldn't be afraid to go after what he wanted. Her grandfather used to say that.

"We were married and we got divorced. See, no happy ending," she told him. She was happily distracted when their entrée arrived.

Opening up wasn't easy for her, another fact to file in his mental database, Sean thought. He was learning more about Tate Dennison than he'd anticipated. Then again, he reminded himself that she wasn't a part of the plan; she was definitely outside the box for him. Whether that was a good or bad thing, he'd yet to decide.

For right now, he could tell that Briana's father had never taken her to nice dinners or treated her like she was special. Nor any other man, for that matter. Hence the reason she was so against him doing just that. So why did he insist on doing it? Because from the moment he'd set foot in her office and seen her first dimpled smile, he knew she was special indeed.

Chapter 8

"You have a really nice family," Tate said when they were once again in Sean's car.

They'd picked up Briana from the Big House and were headed back to her apartment. The cheerful little girl was sleeping soundly in her new car seat, which looked oddly at home in Sean's sports car.

"Thanks. I like them," he said with a slight chuckle.

He hadn't missed how nervous she was when they entered the Big House. And when they could hear Briana's laughter floating through the spacious house, she'd tensed a little more.

"Your mother is very down-to-earth," she continued saying as Sean drove through the dark Miami streets.

"Did you think she wouldn't be?"

Out of the corner of his eye, he saw her shrug. "I

don't know what I thought. I mean, I've never met a family like yours."

"And what type of family do you have?"

The initial answer was her silence. She definitely did not like talking about herself. But Sean had no intention of stopping until he knew everything he could about her. If that took more dinner dates and more babysitting requests from his family, then that's what would happen.

"I have two older sisters. They live in Maryland. My mother died when I was thirteen so my father had the burden of raising three sassy and stubborn girls on his own. Well, not necessarily on his own. When my mother passed, we moved into my father's childhood home with my grandfather."

"Sounds like a pretty close-knit family. Just like mine."

She shook her head. "No. We're not like your family. Or at least we weren't." She took a deep breath. "We weren't a bad family, that's not what I mean at all. Actually, my father and my grandfather were very loving and supportive, especially when we grew up and decided what career paths to take."

"And how did they feel about you moving all the way down here and taking their granddaughter? I know my mother would flip if she had grandkids and either of us thought about moving them to a different state. Whew!" he said, shaking his own head. "Hell hath no fury like Janean Donovan."

Sean laughed thinking about his mother's reaction, but he knew deep down it was no laughing matter. Janean would really be livid at such an arrangement.

"They may have been upset if they'd known," she said quietly, but Sean heard her loud and clear.

"Your family doesn't know where you are?"

She didn't answer verbally, only shook her head. He almost ran right through a red light as he turned to see her reaction to the question. Pressing harder on the brakes, his fingers flexed on the steering wheel. "Why didn't you tell them?"

"It's a long story," she said.

"I've got all night," he said.

She shook her head again just as the light switched to green.

"I don't want to talk about it." This reply came more adamantly.

"Does it have anything to do with Briana's father?"

"What part of 'I don't want to talk about it' did you not understand?" she said in a burst of temper.

Reluctantly, Sean let his mouth clamp shut on his next retort and kept it that way until he'd parked in front of her apartment building. By the time he'd climbed out of the car and walked around to the passenger side, Tate was already out and pushing her seat back so she could reach the car seat.

"I'll get her," she said briskly.

"No," Sean told her, taking her arm and moving her gently to the side. "I'll take her in."

She was angry, but Sean couldn't tell if that was because he'd asked her too many questions or because of the subject of those questions. This marked the second time this evening he'd asked about Briana's father and she'd clamped up with a frown that said this was a dangerous subject.

As he unsnapped the harness that held Briana in the car seat, he couldn't help but stare down into her angelic face. What kind of man could walk away from her? At two years old, she was already beautiful, and Sean felt like he was suddenly falling head over heels for her. When he scooped her out of the seat, he held her close to his chest as he backed out of the car. Her scent was fresh and intoxicating. A scent he wasn't familiar with but one he could quickly get used to. On instinct, he turned his face to her cheek and kissed her softly.

Behind him he heard the car door slam. By the time they came to the double glass doors that led to the lobby, Tate had come around to walk in front of him. She opened the door and held it for him. Her apartment was on the third floor, so she led the way to the elevators and pressed the button. On one shoulder she held Briana's diaper bag. Her arms were folded across her chest—a chest that was more than ample, as he'd been treated to an irresistible view all night. He didn't know the designer of her dress, because fashion wasn't his thing. What he did know—no, correction, what he prayed—was that she had a closet full of them, because she looked great in it. When they stepped into the elevator, Sean couldn't tell which one of these two had begun wrapping their fingers around his heart first, but he knew for a fact that he wasn't finished with either one of them.

"Thank you," she said tightly when they were once again inside her apartment. "It seems like I'm always saying that to you."

"You don't have to," he told her when he stood in her living room. He'd noted she wasn't big on furniture—not adult furniture, that is. There was no mistaking that a baby lived here, from the corner with her playpen to the opposite corner that held a bright green tub of toys. The living room was connected to the small dining area with its table and two chairs and high chair that held more stuffed toys.

"Which way is her room? I'll put her to bed," he asked.

"You don't have to," she said, mimicking him and then smiling at the coincidence. "I can take her from here."

"Let's try this again. I'd like to put Briana to bed, Tate. I'm not going to hurt her."

Her questioning gaze kept him still, along with the fact that she hadn't told him where Briana's room was.

"What are you afraid of? That someone's going to take her from you?"

"No!" she said quickly. "Her room's this way."

Sean walked behind her and entered another baby haven. From the Minnie Mouse border that stretched around the walls to the pretty pink canopy that covered the brown crib, he knew instantly that the child that lived in this room was loved.

"You have to change her first and put on her pajamas," he heard her say.

Sean had never changed a baby in his life. But that didn't mean he couldn't do it. There was nothing he couldn't do. That had been his mentality for so long that his fingers were already moving to remove the baby's clothes before his mind knew what he was doing. Tate came up beside him, her soft perfume permeating the air, and Sean felt a clutching in his chest that was becoming all too familiar when he was around these two. She handed him a diaper.

"Tape's on the sides. Place this one under the old one to avoid mistakes."

"Mistakes?" he asked, looking at her.

She nodded.

"Oh yeah, mistakes." He did as she said, placing the new paper beneath Briana's bottom. He stripped the tape from the old diaper, removed it and fastened the new one in place. Painless, he thought with a smile to himself.

"Pajamas," she said.

He took the pajamas out of her hand. They were lavender with yellow teddy bears. Cute, he thought as he slipped her feet inside first, then her arms. He was snapping it up the center when Tate reached over the crib and activated some sort of musical device. It was soft and low and sent reflections of slow-moving clouds along the ceiling of the canopy.

"She won't stay asleep in the crib without hearing the music first," Tate told him as she moved toward the door.

Sean stood there for a few more moments, looking down at the quietly sleeping baby. He could do this again, wanted to do this again.

"Goodnight, Sean," Tate said from the doorway.

He cleared his throat and moved to the door. "She's a wonderful child, Tate. You did good."

She smiled. After a night of dodging his questions, looking worried and uncomfortable, she'd finally smiled.

And those dimples reached right inside Sean's chest to grip his heart, fast and hard.

"She's my best achievement," she said finally.

"She's pretty fantastic."

He lifted a hand to her cheek and let it sit there as he stared at her. Words weren't coming as fast as he would like, and that wasn't normal for Sean. He always knew what he wanted to say and when he wanted to say it. But at this moment he didn't.

"You should go," she said, taking a step back so that his hand dropped from her face.

"What are you afraid of, Tate? Is it me? Or is it any man?"

"I'm not afraid of you or anyone else. I just don't want what you do. I work for your company, and I'm grateful for this new opportunity you're affording me. But that's all there is between us. All there will ever be."

Could such a cold blow come from a woman with such warm eyes and a mouth that had just been smiling at him? Obviously it could.

"So you're afraid of getting involved with the boss?" he said, amending his question.

"I'm not afraid of anything," she snapped.

"Really?"

He moved closer and she backed right into the hallway wall until there was nowhere else for her to go. Her arms shifted from her sides to a defensive stance folded over her chest. She took that stance often enough that he was beginning to read the warning signs. But they weren't going to stop him, not this time. He pressed even closer. "Are you sure you're not afraid of me? Of what I make you feel?" he whispered, lowering his face closer to hers.

"You don't make me feel anything," she said, but her breath was soft and airy.

"I don't make you feel like you want to make love? Like you want my hands on your body, my lips on yours?"

She shook her head, her lips clamping tight as she swallowed.

"Prove it," he said, touching his lips lightly to hers. "Prove you're not afraid."

His lips slid along hers once more.

"How?" she breathed against him.

"Kiss me. Just this once, Tate, kiss me."

With slow, even strokes his tongue moved along her lower lip, touched the crease between and then swiped over her top lip.

"Sean," she whispered.

And he took that as his cue. Delving deep and without remorse, his tongue touched hers in a scorching connection. His lips covered hers, his head slanted, hands grasping her shoulders. He kissed her like he'd never kissed any other woman in his life. Sinking, floating, sinking, drowning—that's what it felt like to kiss Tate Dennison. She was pulling him in deeper even though her hands hadn't touched him at all. Her head tilted opposite his, until her mouth was opening willingly, her tongue taking wantonly. And he indulged—damn did he indulge—in the sweetest torture he'd ever endured.

When her palms flattened against his chest, Sean pushed further, plunged deeper and was rewarded with her hungry moan as she pressed her body against his. He'd known it. And it wasn't just his Donovan ego, which he was well aware that he possessed. No, this was true and honest desire. Tate wanted him as badly as he wanted her. She was proving that to him at this very moment.

Then she was pushing him away. Her palms pressed so hard against his chest that he was dazed for a few seconds.

"There. I proved it. Now you can go," she said and slipped out of his grasp.

In a move that was most likely a disgrace to the men in his family, Sean stood there in a haze of thwarted desire. He couldn't move, as his heart thumped against his chest. Then he gave himself a mental kick and headed for the front door, where she was already standing.

"I had a wonderful time tonight," he said as he moved past her, close, but not close enough to touch. When he stood on the other side of the threshold, he turned to face her. "You had a good time, too. You can admit that tomorrow after you've had a chance to really think about it."

"It's just business between us, Sean. That's all there can be," she said adamantly.

But she refused to meet his gaze. And in that one act, she admitted more than he'd ever need her to say.

"There can be whatever we want. We're both consenting adults. You just proved that. Good night, Tate."

He was gone before she could respond.

And before either of them could realize they hadn't been alone.

Tate had no idea what time it was when she heard Briana crying through the baby monitor for the second time that night. Throwing back the comforter, she decided she'd bring Briana into the bed with her for the duration of the night. Getting up every hour or so was going to make waking in the morning a task she didn't want to deal with.

She was cooing when she scooped Briana into her arms. Pressing a cheek to her baby's forehead, Tate checked for a fever. She'd done this twice already and was rewarded by the same result. No fever. Briana was dry and she'd had a bottle of milk the last time Tate had awakened with her. So all should be well. Still, her daughter had a steady whimper that was beginning to concern Tate.

"Maybe you're getting another tooth," Tate said, heading into her bedroom.

Briana's head lay against her chest, whining as Tate slipped beneath the covers and lay back in her bed. She rocked Briana and hummed the lullaby that was on the mobile in her crib. And just when Briana had quieted and Tate was finally drifting off to sleep, the crash came.

It was loud and scared Tate right out of her sleep. She screamed, and Briana jumped and wailed. Glass shattered and Tate immediately reached for her cell phone. Punching 911 on the dial pad as quickly as she could, she kept Briana close and leaned to the side of the bed to collect her softball bat. It sounded as if it were the window in Briana's room, but Tate wasn't going to go and investigate. If she'd been alone she probably would have, but with her crying baby next to her, she wasn't about to risk Briana's safety.

"Someone's breaking into my house," she told the operator and rattled off her address.

Through the wall she heard cursing and furniture being knocked over. She held Briana tightly in one arm, the bat in the other hand. She was rocking and trying to soothe her child, when her own heart was hammering in her chest. Footsteps sounded in the small hallway, and Tate knew the intruder was now headed her way. With their safety in mind, she lay Briana in the center of the bed. It broke her heart to see her baby crying so loudly and hard enough to make her little cheeks turn red, but she couldn't very well defend them both by sitting on the bed. She gripped the bat in both hands and walked slowly toward the door. When she was close enough, she locked it. Then she searched for something to put up against it.

She looked over at the bed, and Briana was attempting to scooch her body right off the side. When Tate took a step to grab her, there was a banging at the door. Tate jumped and held on to the bat even tighter. She stood with her legs spread slightly apart, ready to swing at whoever came through that door. Then she heard sirens and felt a small wave of relief. More cursing sounded as fists banged against her door so hard it shook the hinges.

"Get the hell out of my house!" she screamed on impulse, moving closer to the door. "I've got a gun, and the minute you walk through that door I'm shooting!"

The door shook again, this time as if it had been kicked.

"C'mon, you bastard," she said, holding the bat like she was about to hit the game-winning home run.

There was more knocking, but it sounded farther off. The front door. She heard mumbled talking just before another crash sounded. Tate felt something on her leg and almost jumped right out of her skin. She almost cried when she looked down to see that Briana had waddled her way over to her and was now extending her arms so Tate could pick her up.

And that she did. She held her daughter tight against her as tears stung her eyes.

"Police! Anybody in here? This is the police!"

Tate heard the yelling but still didn't move. How did she know for sure it was the police? Maybe the intruder had switched his tactics. She wasn't opening that door.

It didn't matter, because in a few seconds it was kicked in, the sound of splintering wood echoing in the room. She pushed Briana to her left side and lifted the bat in her right hand. There was no way she could get a good swing in this position, but Tate vowed she'd do whatever it took to defend her daughter.

In a blur, uniforms entered the room, guns in the air, arms extended.

"Don't move! Don't move!" they yelled.

"I live here," Tate stuttered. "I called…you."

There was clicking and audible releases of breath as arms were lowered and the officers came a little closer.

"Are you hurt, ma'am?"

"No," Tate said, shaking her head.

Another officer came to her side, wrapped his fingers around her wrist. "You can let it go now."

"What?" she asked, her voice sounding far off.

"The bat. Let it go, ma'am," he instructed.

Tate looked at the bat and sighed. "Oh yeah." She released her hold and the officer took the bat from her.

"Just you and your baby here, ma'am?" the officer standing in front of her asked.

She nodded.

"Okay, why don't we get you out of here."

"No. No. I live here," she was telling them.

"We know, ma'am. But this is a crime scene now. We have to investigate. There's a social worker on the way, so you can talk to her and she'll find you someplace to stay tonight."

"But I…this is my…" Tate didn't know what to say.

All she knew for sure was that Briana was okay. She was still crying in Tate's arms, but she was with her and she was okay.

Chapter 9

"So, are we meeting with the newest addition to our television show today?" Parker asked, walking into Sean's office with Savian and Dion right behind him.

Sean had been sitting at his desk, computer on, papers from a file strewn across his desk, a cup of tepid coffee to his right. He hadn't been doing a bit of work. The only thing he'd been able to think about this morning was Tate. Her smile. Her quick wit. Briana and her chubby cheeks and laughing eyes.

"Who invited you in?" he asked the entourage that had descended on his office.

"You know we don't need an invite," Dion said, leaning against the edge of Sean's desk.

Unlike his brother's office, which looked more like a hotel room with its deep-cushioned guest chairs, working table with six less comfortable chairs, mini refrigerator and water machine, Sean's work abode was much more formal. He had a big office, of course, but his furniture leaned more toward the functional than the comfortable. The modern design made the most use of the space while allowing plenty of shelves to store his older volumes of the magazine as well as the manuals with their distribution history. His meeting table was round, with four high-backed chairs. He did have a water machine and refrigerator, he just rarely used them.

Parker had already taken a seat in front of his desk, his long legs extended and crossed at the ankle. Savian, who surpassed even Sean in seriousness, unbuttoned his suit jacket and sat down, his features as stoic as his cool demeanor.

"Did you schedule the meeting yet?" Dion asked. "I mean, a second meeting, since we already heard about the one that took place last night."

"The one at which I'm sure only a minimal amount of business was conducted, if any," Parker added with a chuckle.

He should have known. Nothing happened in his family without everyone knowing. Sean pinched the bridge of his nose and shifted forward to lean his elbows on his desk.

"Oh no, he's worried about something," Dion said with a groan. He lifted Sean's coffee cup then put it back down with a frown. "You need to stay away from this stuff. Caffeine's bad for the nerves."

"I'm not worried, and my caffeine intake is just fine," Sean answered.

"So what's the status?" Savian asked. "I'd like to set up a development meeting with all the key players soon.

We were hoping to have everything squared with 'Ask Jenny' this week."

"She's on board. We'll need a new contract drawn up for her, one that includes child care and health care expenses."

Savian frowned. "We provide health care for all our employees. Always have."

Sean nodded. "I know, but I want to make sure it's included in this new contract as well. Also, the child care. None of that cafeteria-plan crap. We need to pay for hers in full. She has an infant attending day care. Working on the show as well as keeping up with the column is going to require a shift in her work hours. I don't want her to stress about child care in the process."

"She'll get a hefty raise to do the show," Parker said. "She can use that for her child care."

Sean was already shaking his head. "No. I want this to be a separate contract, not attached to her employment at the magazine. So she's not getting a raise, she's getting an entirely different salary."

"Wow, being very generous with this one, aren't you?" Parker asked.

When Sean opened his mouth to speak, Dion held up a hand to halt him.

"Before you say anything, you should know my wife came home last night rambling about this adorable little girl she watched for you. By the time I was in the car on my way to work, Mom was calling to ask if I could talk to you about bringing Tate and…what's her name?"

Sean sighed. "Briana."

"Yeah, Briana, to the house again. She made several more comments about when Lyra and I were going to give her a grandchild as precious as Briana."

Parker was smiling from ear to ear. Savian had the decency to put his hand up over his mouth, pretending to brush down his close-cut mustache to cover the fact that he was grinning as well.

"I think we've already crossed the personal line," Dion finished. "Just in case you were thinking about taking the denial route."

"No," Sean replied automatically. "I wasn't thinking of taking that route." He rubbed his hands down his face and gave up the pretense.

"We had a great time at dinner. Yes, I like her on a personal level. So yes, I'm trying to look out for her in the business arena as well. Satisfied?"

"We can't just give her whatever she wants because you want to sleep with her," was Savian's cool response.

Sean's icy glare was quick, his tone lethal. "I do not just want to sleep with her. And I can negotiate her contract any way I see fit."

"The board has to approve it," Savian retorted, without even blinking an eye at Sean's quick show of temper.

"Time out," Parker said, making a T with his hands. "He's not asking for a million-dollar contract, Savian. She's already getting health care within the scope of her employment here at the magazine. We can just include a clause that says if anything should happen to said employment, this contract will pick up full-coverage health care."

"And add child care when no one else is getting it? Is that fair?" Savian asked.

It was Dion's turn to intervene. "Nobody that we're offering a television contract to has had child-care issues," he told Savian. "We should continue to negotiate contracts on a case-by-case basis and not get into what we are and aren't supplying for everyone else."

"If the company doesn't pay her child care, I will." The words were out before Sean could really consider them. He sat back in his chair and let them sink in. He never said what he didn't mean. Ever. This time was no different.

"It'll be taken care of," Dion said in a tone that ended any further argument. "Now, is she on board with this personal thing?"

"She's not exactly banging on my door to get to the second date," he said with a wry chuckle. "The whole boss/employee thing seems to be an issue for her."

"As it should be," Savian replied.

"Savian, man, you need to get laid," Parker said.

Savian frowned at his older brother. "Unlike you guys, I have more important things on my mind."

"That just confirms you aren't getting any." Dion laughed.

"I think she's got some history that's holding her back," Sean offered, because these men were his closest friends. He could trust each of them—even Savian— and depend on them to be totally honest with him about anything.

"Oh boy, history's never good," Parker said.

"You should know," Savian added. "That's why you're divorced now."

Parker didn't frown and he didn't take another jab at his brother. The subject of his young marriage and quickie divorce wasn't one they broached lightly. And judging from the look on Parker's face, they weren't going to discuss it now.

"What kind of history?" Dion asked. "Let me guess. Baby daddy?"

"I believe so. I'm thinking about having Trent take a look into her past."

Savian shook his head. "Dangerous territory having a woman's background checked out. Especially when it's a woman you plan to sleep with and hire at the same time."

Nobody denied that. But Sean didn't give a damn. For him, the end definitely justified the means.

"She doesn't have to know," he said.

Savian had another response, not that anyone was surprised. "That's right, bring dishonesty into the new relationship as well. Why not just ask her what happened and be done with it?"

"I tried that, and she clammed up. Twice. That's how I know something's going on there," he told them.

"That definitely sounds like she's keeping secrets," Parker said.

"And she's got her guard up so high I'm practically climbing walls just to get a smile." But when he got one, he was blown away, every time.

His desk phone buzzed and Sean pressed the intercom button. "Yes, Gayle?"

"You wanted to know when Ms. Dennison came in. Her assistant just called to say she's not coming in today—some type of family emergency."

His finger slammed against the button.

"Guess that means we're not meeting today," Savian said with a sigh.

Sean was already out of his chair, pulling his suit jacket from the back and slipping his arms in as he walked to the door. "I'm gone for the day. If you need me, call the cell."

* * *

Seeing yellow police tape hanging from the door of Tate's apartment was not something Sean had anticipated. The swirl of anger settling in the pit of his stomach wasn't either. Yet, as he walked inside the already-open door, he felt like he could hit someone. And that wasn't a thought that crossed Sean's mind on a daily basis.

There was an officer in the living room, standing beside Briana's playpen, and he instantly went into defense mode.

"Where's Briana?" he asked the officer.

The female in uniform turned and looked at him. She had a notepad in one hand and a pen in the other, and she took a step closer to him. "And who are you?"

"I'm Sean Donovan," he said. "Where are Briana and Tate?"

He looked around the room, and there didn't seem to be anything out of place, nothing missing. Except for the two females who lived here.

"And how do you know Ms. Dennison?"

He could see the name "Raymond" printed in block letters just beneath her badge, and she had already written his name down and was waiting for what he would say next.

"Ms. Dennison works for me at *Infinity* magazine," he told her. "We had dinner last night and I dropped her off around ten-thirty." Now, whether he was incriminating himself, Sean didn't really care. It was the truth, and he was telling the officer all this in the hopes of getting her to reciprocate.

"You're *that* Sean Donovan?" was her reply.

He wanted to sigh. The last thing he was in the mood

for was someone falling all over themselves trying to impress him because he was *that* Sean Donovan.

"Yes, whatever that means," he said instead. "Can you please tell me where Tate and Briana are?"

She used her pen to point. "They're in the bedroom. Packing, I presume."

Sean didn't allow her to expand on that. He was already walking through the living room, turning down the short hallway and heading toward the room next to Briana's, which he assumed had to be Tate's. All the tension, all the worry that had built up from the moment Gayle had given him the message that Tate was out washed out of him in a gush of a breath. He inhaled again slowly as he saw Tate standing near the dresser gathering clothes and Briana sitting in the center of the bed bending into the suitcase trying to pull out everything her mother had just put inside. Tate was wearing jeans that fit enticingly over her thick thighs and her perfectly rounded bottom. Her hair was pulled into a messy ponytail that gave her a vulnerable quality that called for Sean to help her, be there for her, make this better.

"Pretty little Briana, are you helping Mommy pack?" he said, trying to keep his voice as light as possible— even though anger was just barely simmering inside. What had happened here? Why was she packing, and just where did she think she was going?

He was already on his way to the bed, arms extended to pick Briana up, when Tate jumped on the bed and grabbed her away from him.

"What are you doing here?" she asked, fear and confusion clear on her face. Both pissed Sean off even more.

"I heard you weren't in the office because of a family problem. I came to see if I could help," he told her, standing at the foot of the bed.

Her gaze darted around the room, then just over his shoulder as if she expected or needed someone else to be there. Sean tried valiantly not to take that personally.

"What happened?"

She sighed and sat down on the bed, keeping Briana in a grip so tight the baby squirmed to get away.

"Somebody broke in last night. They came through the window in Briana's room."

Hence the reason she was holding on to her baby as if both their lives depended on it.

Sean moved slowly, coming to sit beside her on the bed. She moved over a little and he decided not to follow her any farther. Extending a hand, he touched Briana's fingers, but he did not touch Tate. She was frightened. He understood that. Just as he understood that the moment he left this apartment he would be calling D&D Investigations to get to the bottom of this incident.

"You got to her in time?"

Tate shook her head, wisps of hair trailing along her cheeks and neck. "No. She'd been cranky all night. I'd gotten up a couple of times with her already. The last time, I figured I'd just bring her in here to sleep with me. Then I heard the window breaking."

"Did they catch the perpetrator?" he asked, already knowing the answer. If they'd caught him, there wouldn't be a cop out in the living room and Tate probably wouldn't be packing.

"No," she said in a low whisper.

Briana reached for him, and Sean extended his arms to her. Tate hesitated, her gaze going to Sean's.

"She's okay, Tate. I'm not going to hurt her or you," he said solemnly.

Her lips compressed and she closed her eyes, releasing her hold on Briana. "I've been a nervous wreck all day. The cops have been here since four this morning, dusting for prints and looking around outside. I thought they'd be gone by now, but they said since nothing was taken they found it strange that the guy would break a window to get in instead of picking the lock."

Sean nuzzled Briana's neck, loving the feel of her baby-soft skin against his. "Impulsive, erratic—that's what they're probably thinking. Not something that was planned." Sean was glad that the police were performing an in-depth investigation.

"I don't care if it was planned or not. It doesn't make me feel better," she said.

"So you're packing because…?" he asked.

"One of the detectives said it might be a good idea to get away for a few days. I can't afford to take a vacation, so I'm just going to find a hotel for me and Briana to stay at for a week."

Not if he had anything to say about it.

"You'll stay with me. Get your stuff together and we'll pack up the cars and head over now."

"No!" she said adamantly, standing up to stare at him like he'd lost his mind. "I can't stay with you."

Chapter 10

Why she'd even tried to argue, Tate had no idea. Sean Donovan was one stubborn man. As she'd argued with him, he'd calmly played with Briana while going from the baby's room to the living room, transporting her toys and breaking down her playpen. After he'd simply stared at her and asked, "Are you finished?"

No, damn it! She hadn't been finished. She was willing to bet he hadn't even been listening to her, as his mind was already made up.

"This is not a good idea," she said as they pulled up to a white gate and waited while Sean swiped a card and was allowed in.

She'd left her car at the apartment—that was another argument he'd won. Sean had talked to the officer who was still at her apartment. He mentioned the break-in of her car the other day and how she thought they might be connected. So they left the car to make it look like she was still home, in the event the assailant came back. She supposed that was a good enough reason but really didn't like having her independence taken away so blithely.

"It's the best option for right now. Relax," he told her.

How could she relax? She hadn't lived with a man in a year, and that man had been her husband. Sean was not.

"I can still go to a hotel," she said as he parked the car.

When the vehicle was stopped and Sean had clicked off his seatbelt, he turned in his seat to face her.

"Look, I'd really like for you and Briana to stay with me. The attack on your car and the break-in must be connected, which means this person is looking for you personally. As your employer, I'm very concerned for your safety as well as the safety of Briana."

He sounded so sincere, so compassionate, and oh so smooth. If she kept staring into his soothing bedroom eyes, Tate was sure she'd strip right here for him if he asked. Instead, she took a steadying breath and tried to make the best possible decision for her and her daughter.

"We're not staying here long," was her reply.

He nodded and stepped out of the car. She carried Briana while he carried their other bags, saying he'd come down later for the rest.

It was early afternoon and Briana hadn't had lunch yet. So when they arrived at his door she was beginning to whine. Tate was cooing against her daughter's ear when she walked through the door, telling her she was getting ready to fix her lunch and then she could have a nice nap.

His home was beautiful. She shouldn't have been surprised—he was a Donovan, after all. It didn't have the grab-you-by-the-throat-and-strangle-you-with-hospitality-and-warmth feel of his parents' house, or what they called the Big House. No, Sean's home, from what she could see so far, had a more contemporary appeal. Without question, it said high-rise Miami Beach, with its floor-to-ceiling windows and crisp white-tiled floors. The walls in the foyer were also a brilliant white, which instantly had Tate worrying. Briana was at the age where she liked to touch things, and everything she touched inevitably picked up her smudged finger-prints. She could see these walls as a blank canvas for her inquisitive toddler.

"The kitchen is this way," he said, leading her down a long hallway.

On the way there were open doors and more sunlight spilling in from windows. Her sandals clicked lightly on the floors as she followed him into a spacious kitchen decorated in muted colors. She noted that it was extremely orderly for a man who lived alone.

"I'll let you get her settled. I have some phone calls to make," he told her.

As he walked past, he rubbed a hand over Briana's head. Almost like a father would do. When he was gone, Tate sighed and then slapped a palm against her fore-head. Sean Donovan was just being nice. He was not, nor would he ever be, Briana's father.

Lord only knew where her father was.

"You're right," Trent Donovan said through the phone. "It's got to be connected."

Sean had closed himself in his room and called Dion.

Once he told his brother what had happened, they'd immediately hooked Trent up on a conference call.

"So somebody's stalking her?" Sean asked, his throat constricting at the very thought.

"I don't know if you could say stalking, but somebody's definitely trying to get to her. What else do you know about her past?"

"Just that she just moved here with her daughter, and Briana's father is not in the picture," he informed them.

"That's not much to go on," Dion said. "We can pull her personnel file to see what's on her resume."

"I want security on her and Briana at all times," Sean told them, but he was greeted by silence on the line.

"She's staying with you and you want security on her?" Trent asked.

"He's interested in her," Dion offered.

Sean let them take a moment to laugh and make their snide comments. He was probably the last Donovan they thought would fall for a woman with a kid, or any woman at all, since he'd remained focused on work and family for so long. No, Savian would be the absolute last. He felt a world better at that thought.

"Look, I don't want anything to happen to them. Is something wrong with that?"

"No. Not at all," Trent said. "Man, I'm just glad to see you taking action for a change instead of worrying and overthinking everything."

If he only knew, Sean thought. He'd been overthinking Tate Dennison since the day he walked into her office. And after their kiss last night, the one that neither of them had mentioned at all today, he knew he wouldn't think of anything else but getting his hands on her again.

"A friend of mine lives in the area. I'll give him a call. If he's available he'll be in touch with you tonight. I presume you've got her covered for the night," Trent said with a chuckle.

Dion joined in. "Yeah, I'm sure he's got her covered tonight."

"Very funny, both of you. We'll stay in tonight. I don't want them going out and chancing anything."

What Sean realized he wanted for Tate and Briana was much more than he'd ever dreamed of with another woman. He wondered what it was about this one that had clicked into place so soon and so decisively.

After hanging up with his brother and his cousin, Sean stood in his bedroom staring out the window at the Miami scenery. He thought about his parents, about their long, love-filled marriage; about his brother and his new wife, and the other Donovan men of his family. None of them had planned to fall in love and settle down, at least not at the exact moment it happened. He shouldn't feel concerned about this new development in his life. And actually, he didn't. But he knew Tate was.

Chapter 11

"You make it look so easy," Sean said as he watched Tate put a sleeping Briana into the Pack and Play crib they'd set up in the second-floor guest room.

Usually his guests used the first-floor bedroom, but he'd wanted them closer to him. Tate had unpacked earlier while Briana napped after her lunch. The room looked totally different than it had just that morning, he noted. There were baby things all over. And now he watched the woman who'd enchanted him through another dinner that night, performing what looked like her normal nightly ritual with her daughter.

And Sean realized he was sinking fast.

She shrugged, her long hair falling freely around her shoulders. "I'm used to it now," was her reply.

"She usually sleeps all night?"

Tate nodded. "Except for last night."

"We're going to find out what's going on, Tate. I don't want you to worry about that."

When she looked up at him Sean's breath caught as the dimly lit room made her skin look almost golden and her eyes look like simmering pools. "How can I not worry? Somebody's after me and my baby."

He moved closer until he was standing directly in front of her. Lifting his hands, he grasped her shoulders and pulled her slowly until her body brushed against his. "You're safe now. I'm not going to let anything happen to either one of you."

She began shaking her head. "But you're my boss. You don't know us at all. I don't understand why you'd go through all this trouble for us."

"Because of this," he said, wrapping his arms around her. "Because of what I feel when I'm with you. And what I know you feel, too."

She was shaking her head again.

"You're going to develop a neck condition if you keep that up," he said.

She stopped instantly, and Sean used a finger to lift her chin. "Does it seem quick? Yes. Would I have believed I'd be so interested in a woman I'd just officially met days ago? Probably not." He shrugged. "But I've never been one to second-guess what I feel. I go with my gut. Always."

"And let me guess," she said with a smirk, "you're never wrong."

"I wouldn't say never. But my track record's looking pretty good so far," he said honestly.

She smiled, and it was as if someone had flipped a switch inside his body. The pleasant warmth he'd felt just holding her escalated tremendously.

"I'm not used to this," she said, her voice trembling.

"Believe me, neither am I."

Holding her felt too right—it felt perfect, to be exact—but a part of Sean wanted more. The finger that was on her chin traced a line along her jaw and then touched her bottom lip lightly.

"We can't ignore this," he said softly, watching as her eyes grew darker with his touch.

"No. I don't think we can," she admitted on a deep sigh. "I wanted to. I really did. But I've always been a realist."

"It shows in your writing." He couldn't help but say that. "It's one of the first things that attracted me to you. There's a brutal honesty in your words. You have no idea what a turn-on an honest woman is."

She laughed. "Really? I don't think a lot of women know that."

"Obviously not."

He couldn't wait another minute. He replaced his finger with his lips, touching hers in a whisper-soft connection. To his continued delight, she didn't flinch or attempt to move away. Just like during their kiss last night, she only melted into his embrace, parting her lips at his insistence. Kissing Tate produced this eerie fog that engulfed both of them as they sank deeper, melding their bodies closer together.

Her arms circled his back, their bodies pressing together tightly. She tilted her head, coming up on her tiptoes to offer him even more. His palms itched to touch her, to feel the heat of her skin against his own. With one hand he grasped her bottom, and the other reached beneath the rim of her T-shirt until he was touching her bare back. Her hand went to the back of his head, pulling him closer, pressing for a deeper kiss.

She was breathless when Sean finally pulled away. He didn't hesitate to lift her into his arms, dropping soft kisses on her forehead, her nose, her cheeks as he carried her into his bedroom.

His bed was huge, even for a man of his six-foot-four, 227-pound frame. It was a king-size mattress on a chocolate-brown leather-covered platform. His sheets and the complementing decor were in ivory. The moment he lay Tate on the satin comforter, her golden complexion and dark eyes became even more vibrant and her body became more alluring.

She moved to take off her shoes, but he pushed her hands away. "I'll do it," he told her. "You just lie there."

It was just after nine in the evening, and there was a full moon that sent slashes of smoky white light through the slits in his blinds. He knelt on the floor in front of the bed and untied each of her shoes, pulling them slowly from her feet. He rubbed her bare soles up to her toes, massaging deeply.

Tate moaned, her head falling back on her shoulders. "That feels divine," she told him.

"Just wait till I really get my hands on you," was his reply.

Leaving her feet for the moment, he vowed it would not be the last foot massage she received from him. He undid the clasp of her jeans, slid the zipper down and then pulled the denim over her thighs and off. His hands whispered over her calves, upward until the soft flesh of her inner thighs warmed his fingertips. Spreading her legs slightly, he touched her juncture, which was covered in a silky fabric that had already grown damp.

She gasped, and he swallowed deeply, forcing himself to take his time. The T-shirt came next in a quick pull over her head. Sean sent up a silent thank-you to the heavens for matching panty-and-bra sets. The same cream-colored silk that graced her center cupped her mouthwatering breasts. On quick assessment, he noticed that it had a front clasp, and he gingerly pushed a finger between her mounds to release it. When they were free, it was his turn to gasp. Dark nipples instantly hardened, and he deftly lowered his head to take one into his mouth.

Spears of lust soared through his body, and his erection pressed against the zipper of his jeans. His hand grasped the second breast, kneading it while his mouth caressed its twin. Then he had to have both hands on her, so he grasped both breasts and pushing them together so his tongue could quickly move from one puckered nipple to the other.

Her fingers clenched tight at the back of his head as Sean's heart pounded wildly in his chest. She whispered his name, and inside he went insane. It was a toss-up between the nervousness of the first time he'd had sex and the best sex he'd ever had. The intensity that rushed through him at this moment was almost overwhelming. What he knew for certain was that he'd never had an erection so hard, so damned persistent.

She grabbed at his shirt, pulling it from the collar in a race to get it over his head. He reluctantly tore his mouth away from her, dipping his head lower and straightening his arms so she could remove the shirt. Her palms feathered over his bare skin, tracing a scorching path from his pectorals down to his stomach.

"It's so damned hot in here," he groaned, his teeth nipping her earlobe.

"That's because you have on too many clothes."

He leaned back on his knees, preparing to unbutton his pants, when she swiped his hands away and undid the button herself, pushing his pants along with his boxers over his hips. It took some maneuvering to get them and his shoes off, and they laughed as their bodies contorted in unseemly positions. When they fell back on the bed, both of them gloriously naked, she slapped a palm on his chest.

"Do you have protection?"

As if she had to ask. Sean didn't respond, only rolled to his side and retrieved a condom from his nightstand. After he'd covered his length with the latex, he stretched over her, pushing her thighs apart, looking down into her lust-filled eyes.

"Never doubt that I'll protect you, Tate. I won't let anything happen to you," he said. And Sean never said what he didn't mean.

He looked so sincere, his deep brown eyes so alluring, like some kind of drug drawing her in. And try as she might, Tate could not resist him. She just couldn't.

So instead of fighting what she knew would be a losing battle, she extended her arms until they once again wrapped around his strong shoulders. There was strength in his touch, in the feel of skin over lean muscles. She found that touching him was intoxicating all by itself. Her fingers practically itched to drum along his skin. She sighed when her hands were clasped behind his head. And when she pulled him down and his lips hovered just over hers, she made her request.

"Take me."

It felt familiar, like a lover returning after a long absence. They fit perfectly, his rhythm—hungry and erotically precise—matched hers exactly. When he moaned, Tate moaned. He filled her so completely that she wondered where he stopped and she began.

Never in her life had sex been this way, and that confused her, because this felt so natural. When he lifted her legs, resting them on his shoulders and thrusting deeper inside her, she couldn't speak, could only grip the sheets tightly and close her eyes. Then she opened them again, because she didn't want to miss one moment of seeing him. His face barely contorted, his jaw locked and strong, eyes piercing and focused solely on her. His lips parted slightly to accommodate the rush of breath. It was as if he were concentrating deeply on her.

Tate didn't know how that should make her feel. What she did know for certain was that this joining was everything she'd ever imagined from a real lover. Not the quick jaunts in bed that she shared with Patrick. This was real, it was adult and it was driving her insane with a still-growing need.

"I can't stop," he said, his voice hoarse with the effort. "You feel so good."

She gripped his biceps and moaned when he hit a particular spot, sending ripples of pleasure up and down her spine. "Yes! You feel good, too."

He put her legs down, scissoring them to the side. She rolled partially, lifting her hips so he could enter her from this new direction.

"Mmmmm," she moaned as his erection pierced her deeper at an angle that felt absolutely amazing.

"More?" he asked.

Hell yes! her mind screamed, but all she could manage was another, "Mmmmhmmm."

After several glorious minutes, Sean pulled out of her gently and lay on his back. His strong hands gripped her hips and pulled her over his body. Tate straddled him instantly, her breath only hitching minutely.

Patrick never liked her on top, said it made her seem wanton and desperate. She'd dismissed the comments about her being too heavy to ride him in lieu of slapping him for them.

When her palms flattened on Sean's stomach, he didn't even flinch. Instead, his hands circled her hips, grasped her buttocks and kneaded. He licked his lips, blew out a deep breath and moaned.

"You feel so good, Tate. In my hands, connected to me, just everywhere."

His words melted around her, wrapping her up like a favorite treat. Lifting herself slightly and touching his still-throbbing length, Tate guided him back inside. Her thighs trembled as she lowered herself onto his thick shaft. His teeth gritted. Finally, he was completely inside her and Tate remained perfectly still, loving the feel of him embedded so deep.

But that wasn't the only feeling she loved. It was the power. As she lifted slightly, let a few inches of him slide from her tight grasp, he hissed, his teeth biting down on his lower lip. There was nothing but pleasure etched over his gorgeously sculpted face—pleasure that she provided. She rocked back gently and then slid down completely. He grabbed her hips tighter. She repeated the up, rock, down motion until he was cursing. Then she pumped faster, moving her hips to the blissful feel of his erection. The friction was fierce and caused her to tremble from its delectability.

When her climax came it was quick and strong and forced her thighs to clench around him, holding them close together until the swirling sensations were complete.

Sean watched with unparalleled pleasure as her head tilted back, her lips parted and she moaned with the force of her release. His hands stilled on her hips, fingers digging deep into her skin. She was beautiful, her skin glistening in the moonlight, her curves begging to be touched. He wanted her again and again, but he also wanted to find his release. Because that would cement what he'd been thinking since she'd climbed on top of him.

It was just like the dream he'd had nights ago—every sensation, every moan, every touch. This was the woman. He'd dreamed of her before he'd met her. Now he'd met her and he'd made love to her. He wouldn't let her go, he knew that without a doubt. The name for the emotion swirling around in his chest eluded him at the moment, but he did not deny it outright. This was different for her—new, fast, doubtful. For him, the man who prided himself on being decisive, it was an absolute.

His release came with that thought, bursting from him in a rush of satisfaction. She collapsed on his chest, her hair tickling his nose. He wrapped his arms around her, holding her close so that their hearts beat in unison.

She was his. Now and forever. That was a fact of which Sean was absolutely certain.

Chapter 12

"How did you cut your hand?"

"With glass," was Patrick Dennison's tight reply. "Just get me a towel, would you?" he yelled at the maid, who, in his estimation, was way too smart for her own good. Giselle was her name, and she was always in his face. Smiling and asking questions, touching his arm or glancing at him from beneath those long, dark lashes she had. He knew what she wanted, what she thought he had to give, and ordinarily he would have been eager to give it to her. But his return to Miami hadn't been planned.

Tate wasn't supposed to be here, but she was. And so he'd had to come.

He hadn't thought about her in months. Hell, to be perfectly honest, Patrick hadn't thought about Tate since the day he'd walked out of their apartment nine months ago. The divorce had been quick and painless—no contest, no reconciliation, just done. She hadn't even asked for child support for the baby. And Patrick hadn't offered a thing. He'd hung around Maryland for a while after that, spending his newly acquired fortune on booze and women. The next part of his plan consisted of long days on some secluded beach and hot, sultry nights with any willing female. Instead he was here, looking for Tate.

The first time he'd seen her had been three days ago at the Excalibur Business Center. He'd thought he was seeing things, because she didn't look the same. Her face appeared softer, her clothes more attractive. This wasn't the woman he'd married who'd worked at the local newspaper and read the obituaries just because. He'd been sitting in the car waiting, which was how he spent most of his time these days. She'd come out of the building talking with another woman, then they'd crossed the street and entered a parking garage.

The next day he'd shown up around the same time and followed her through the garage, noting that she drove the same car she had in Maryland. Now he knew where she lived and where the child went to day care. He didn't really care about the child, not beyond how she fit into his current plan.

"You should maybe see a doctor, señor," Giselle said, wrapping a bathroom towel around his right fist.

"I'm fine," he told her, frowning so hard his temples throbbed.

Briana hadn't been in her crib. He'd watched their apartment at night for the past two days. It faced the back of the building, and there was a Dumpster that put him up just high enough to pull down the fire escape and climb up until he was at their windows. From what he could see, Briana had a pretty room. So did Tate. She'd actually done better for herself than he'd thought she would.

In fact, that's what had surprised him most about seeing her again. He'd been sure she would have run back to her family in Maryland, begging them to forgive her. She'd been so upset about cutting her ties with them, but Patrick was sure it was for the best. Her father and grandfather were meddling geezers who would have bled them dry the moment Patrick came into some money. And her sisters ran their mouths way too much, and they would have been filling Tate's head with all sorts of nonsense about him. Leaving that crazy bunch alone had been a good decision.

Moving to the kitchen sink, he switched on the cold water, unwrapped his hand and thrust it beneath the spray. Tingles of pain rippled through his arm, and he clenched his teeth to keep from yelling out. Most likely there were still pieces of glass in his hand, but he wasn't going to any hospital. That would bring too much attention, and he needed to lay low, at least for a while longer.

"Go get some tweezers," he yelled to Giselle. "And hurry up!"

She moved quickly out of the room. In a hurry to please him, he thought with some satisfaction. That's how cooperative he needed Tate to be.

Tate's internal clock made her stir at a few minutes before six in the morning. This was her normal wake-up time, as it took about an hour and a half to get herself and Briana ready for the day. She'd make her drop-off

at the day care and then head to work and be at her desk
no later than eight-thirty.

When she rolled over and realized she wasn't alone
in bed, she figured her morning routine might need a
little adjusting.

His body was hard as her knee grazed his, her toes
rubbing slightly over his calf. She thought about pulling away but then took a moment just to feel, to savor.
Last night had been outstanding, if that word could even
describe their lovemaking. It had been something out
of a storybook. Not a fairy tale—more like a lustful
tale, she thought with a smile creeping onto her face.

Afterward he'd held her. Moments later he'd gotten
up and asked her to join him in the shower. She had,
because she'd already thrown in the towel on resisting
their attraction. What would happen because of her decision to sleep with her boss, she would just have to deal
with later. She deserved this one night of pleasure and
was profoundly glad she'd partaken.

"That's what I like to wake up to—a beautiful smiling woman," he said, jolting Tate from her thoughts.

Her eyes opened quickly, embarrassment warming
her cheeks.

He touched a finger to her cheek as if he knew the
warmth grew there. More likely he could see a rosy
blush, and Tate tried to look away from him.

"Good morning," he whispered, lifting her face
gently so she was looking at him again.

He came in instantly for a soft kiss on her lips. A
kiss that made her melt all over.

"Good morning," she said when he'd pulled back
slightly.

Then there was a gurgling sound and baby chatter

resonated throughout the room. For a moment, Sean looked perplexed.

"It's Briana," she told him, moving away and throwing the covers off her legs. "I brought the monitor in here last night after, um, after." She was fumbling for words, and she absolutely hated that. So she shut her mouth and moved out of the bed to find her robe. Slipping it and her slippers on, she was about to leave when he grabbed her arm.

He hadn't taken the time to put on a robe, so he stood before her in boxer briefs that did absolutely nothing to hide his morning arousal.

"It's okay," he told her. "I don't mind both my ladies saying good morning."

Both his ladies? No, she warned herself. No. No. No. He didn't mean anything by that. He was just saying it because it seemed to fit the moment. Her response was to smile.

"I'll go get her so we can get ready. We'll use the downstairs bathroom to stay out of your way."

Sean was already shaking his head before she could finish speaking. "You'll use the bathroom up here just as you did last night. You're not in my way. We're both adjusting our morning routines. It'll be fine."

She only nodded, afraid of what might come out of her mouth if she attempted to talk. Tate wanted to refuse again, but she knew it sounded idiotic. After all, she'd slept with the man. Acting like a shy schoolgirl now was just pointless.

"And Tate," he called to her.

She stopped at the door and turned to face him. "Yes?"

"I'll drive us in to work and we can stop at your place this evening to pick up your car."

Again she nodded and then felt like a mute. "That will be fine," she replied and walked away before he could stop her once more.

The ride to the day care and to the office was silent. Sean figured she was gathering her thoughts about the change in their relationship. He wanted to give her that time. Because for him, there was no turning back. He liked this woman, a lot, and he wanted to get to know her and her daughter. If she needed a little peace and quiet to accept that, he was game.

But when they stepped out of his car, he felt he had to at least make his intentions clear.

"I respect your feelings about sleeping with your boss," he began as she collected her things out of the car and then stood to face him.

"Word spreads like wildfire around here," she admitted. "I don't plan on telling anyone about last night or our current living arrangements."

He nodded, figuring that's how she would plan to deal with it. Unfortunately, he wasn't in agreement.

"I don't hide. If I'm sleeping with you, I'm the only person sleeping with you. And you can expect the same from me. To that end, if I'm dating you, that's out in the open. While I'm not a fan of tabloids or office gossip, I'm not in the habit of living my life in secrecy."

She didn't respond immediately, which Sean expected. What she did do shocked him.

"Understood," she said, coming up on tiptoe to kiss him lightly.

He watched her walk toward the elevator in amazement. He'd been poised for an argument, but none had come. This might be one for the record books, he thought. The first time a woman had baffled him.

Tate answered three letters before noon, finding her advice coming quickly and seamlessly to the lovelorn. Actually, the letters she'd selected were all from men asking questions such as, "How can I show my lady she's the only woman I want?" To that she'd replied:

When you look at her, take her hands and tell her exactly how you feel. If you're truly sincere, she'll get the message. It's not in the material things you provide her; any man can buy a gift. It's about being honest with her and being there when she needs you. The simplest way to convince her is to show her.

After she'd finished typing, Tate thought about the dinner Sean had prepared for her last night. It wasn't anything fancy, just homemade spaghetti and meatballs with garlic bread, and she forgot the size of her thighs as she enjoyed two thick slices of bread. He'd sat across from her at the island in the center of his kitchen while Briana sat in her high chair—miraculously eating strings of noodles that Sean had cut into small pieces and put into a bowl in front of her.

"I can't believe she's eating that," she'd said to him, unable to keep the amazement from her voice. "Everything I feed her, she tosses across the room."

He laughed, a deep, rich sound that Tate found very comforting. "Maybe she doesn't want to be fed. She seems like a very independent little lady to me. Just like her mother."

Tate had smiled and continued to eat, wondering how Sean knew more about her daughter than she did. She realized that that wasn't really the case, but Sean had a way about him. A sort of Mr. Fix-it mentality—if he saw a problem, it was his job to fix it. Just like he was fixing her temporary homelessness problem. It reminded her of her grandfather and her father, of how they always seemed to step in to take care of things for her and her sisters when they were growing up. She hadn't realized until that moment how much she'd missed that sort of comfort.

Her cell phone rang, loudly, and her startled fingers clicked across her keyboard. Reaching across her desk to where she usually sat her phone during the day, she looked at the screen. The number was reading unknown again. She didn't want to answer it, because she knew it was going to be another hang-up. Just as she was about to hit the button that would send the call directly to her voice mail, Tate thought of the break-ins and wondered if they were connected. On impulse she answered the phone.

"Hello?"

There was no answer, but someone was on the line. She knew because she could hear them breathing.

"Who is this?" she asked, agitation and fear battling for her heart. "I said who is this?"

Then he laughed. Yes, it was a he. And the laugh was familiar.

"Patrick," she sighed.

He hung up.

Chapter 13

"Sabine put an offer on the table," Dion said the moment Sean walked into his office that afternoon.

He'd received an urgent message to call his brother the moment he stepped out of his meeting with a potential advertiser. Instead of calling him, Sean figured he'd just go see him. He really wanted to ask if Dion had heard anything from Trent on Tate's background check. He'd been thinking about her all morning and all through his meeting. Hopefully he hadn't given Cassidy Cosmetics too much of a good deal because of his unusually distracted demeanor.

Now he was standing at the edge of Dion's desk, feeling his temples start to throb as he reached for the piece of paper Dion held out to him.

"Thirty million dollars for *Infinity* and shares into DNT," Dion told him.

"Damn it!" Sean cursed, his fingers tightening on the paper, threatening to crumple it up and toss it across the room. On second thought, he did precisely that.

The paper bounced off the window and fell to the floor behind Dion's desk.

Dion chuckled. "My sentiments exactly."

Sean took a deep, steadying breath and then pinched the bridge of his nose as he gathered his thoughts. "We're still ahead of her by a fifteen-percent margin. This is a bold-ass move on her part."

"She's obviously serious about making a deal. But here's my question. Why?"

"Because she's a controlling bitch. Did you doubt that?" Sean asked as he began pacing.

Dion shook his head. "No. There's got to be something else. Something personal. Why *Infinity?* Why now? And where'd she get all this money? You said yourself that *Onyx* isn't doing better than we are, and even we got hit hard when the economy slumped. So how is it that she has all this ready capital?"

In his mind, Sean reread Sabine's financial records. None of the accounts he remembered seeing had that type of money, even combined.

"You think she has an investor?" he asked, immediately ticking off names in his mind.

Who else would be interested in *Infinity,* or owning a piece of the DNT empire? On a whole, DNT was worth more than six hundred million dollars. That's an amount that would acquire enemies. Enemies that would like nothing better than to see them fold.

"I think it's highly unlikely that a lowly porn star is masterminding this deal all by herself. Where did you get her financial records?"

"There's a guy that works at *Onyx,* in the mailroom. He contacted me a few months ago, said he'd seen my name on a bunch of emails and was wondering if I could use some information."

"Are you paying him?" Dion asked.

Sean stopped pacing and stared at his brother. "Are you crazy? No, I'm not paying him. I told him to get lost. Then the information just started showing up. And last time I checked there was no law against reading mail that's addressed to you."

Dion nodded. "I guess you're right. Even though you're not the lawyer in the family," he added with a chuckle.

No, Sean thought, a thin smile touching his own lips. The lawyer in the Donovan family was their cousin Ben, Matthew's brother, and he lived and practiced in Las Vegas.

"No. I'm not the lawyer. But I can't stop the guy from sending me mail."

"What's this guy's name?"

"Fred Mackley. I kept all the envelopes as well as the contents."

Dion nodded. "Okay. I'll contact Legal today just to make sure we're in the clear on that end. But I still want to find out where she's getting this money."

Sean agreed. "I'll call Trent."

"Good."

Sean turned to leave Dion's office, and his brother was picking up his phone. Then he stopped and said, "Oh, how was staying in last night?"

He should have known Dion wouldn't let that go.

"It was just fine, thank you very much," was his tight but good-natured reply.

* * *

The minute Sean walked in to his office, he sighed. His phone call to Trent would have to wait.

"Hi, Mom," he said, going to the chair where Janean Donovan sat in an impeccable coral-colored pantsuit.

He kissed her cheek and then accepted the kiss she planted on his.

"Hello to you," she said with a smile.

His mother was a beautiful woman with eyes that saw everything, carefully glossed lips that smiled even when she wanted to cuss someone out and high cheekbones that gave away her Native American heritage.

He moved behind his desk, taking off his jacket before sitting down. "What brings you down here today? And in my office? Regan and Lyra are on the fourth floor."

"I know what floor they're on, Sean. Just because I don't work here doesn't mean I don't know what's going on in this building."

He nodded. Of course she knew what was going on thirty miles away from her house. The building belonged to the Donovans, which meant Janean made it her business.

"I'm not looking for Regan or Lyra. They were at the house the other night, remember?"

Okay, so this was about the other night. The babysitting. Sean was betting his mother wanted to know more about Tate and Briana.

"I remember."

"You also came to the house that night. Had a lovely young woman with you, too. What was her name again?"

He felt like he was being reprimanded long before

Janean had even begun with her purpose. Folding his hands in front of him, he did as he used to when he was a child. Answer her questions quickly and concisely and pray that that would get the ordeal over with faster.

"Her name is Tate Dennison. She works as a columnist for the magazine."

Janean nodded. Her dark brown hair was pulled back so that heavy curls hung to her neck. Her full face was perfectly made up with only the slightest enhancement around the eyes and mouth. She sat with her back straight, head held high, just as she'd raised her sons to do. And when she looked at him with her light brown eyes, she saw things he knew nobody else did.

"And?"

"And I took her to dinner to discuss her column being a part of the magazine television show. Parker suggested it a while ago. The ratings for the column have grown tremendously, so I thought it was time to put that in motion."

She nodded once more, folding her fingers together similar to the way he had his. Fading sunlight filtered through the window, catching the huge diamond on her left hand that his father had given her for their thirtieth wedding anniversary.

"Do you find babysitters for all your employees?"

There were two ways he could handle this: continue with the question-and-answer session or just tell her what she wanted to hear. Sean really wanted to call Trent to ask about Sabine, as well as to find out any news about Tate's background. So he was ready to get this over with as quickly as possible.

"Tate's not just an employee," he started off. Then he paused to make sure what he was going to say was actually the right thing to say. The last thing he wanted was for his mother to go off and start planning another wedding, when he was just getting to know the woman.

"I like her a lot and I like her daughter. They're having a difficult time right now, so I offered to let them stay at my place."

Janean, who did not shock easily, raised a questioning eyebrow when he was finished. "Well," she said, releasing her fingers and rubbing her hands over her lap.

"What kind of difficulties are they having? Nothing that's giving you difficulties, I hope."

Sean shook his head. "Someone broke into her car here in the garage, so I took her to pick up her daughter and had the car windows repaired. Then her house was broken into. She wanted to go to a hotel, but I suggested they stay with me."

"So you could take care of them yourself," she finished for him.

"Yes," he answered honestly, because she would have known he was lying otherwise. Besides, not telling his mother the truth was something Sean did not do often, if ever.

"That means you care about her and her child."

"I do." He admitted that also.

"I see." Janean continued to assess her son. "Where's the baby's father?"

"I don't know."

"But you plan to find out?"

He nodded.

"I know I don't have to tell you this, because you're totally different from your brother, but I'm going to say it anyway to ease my own conscience."

Oh, boy, here it comes, he thought. "Children are

not toys, Sean. They're very impressionable, and if that child doesn't have a father in her life, she'll latch on to you quicker than she would a bottle of milk."

He was about to say something, but she held up a hand to stop him.

"Let me finish." She nodded and he did the same. "Single mothers are not to be played with. They, for one reason or another, have already been through enough. You never know when you'll be the one she snaps on."

She took a deep breath. "With that said, I know you're a good man. And from what I've seen of Ms. Dennison, she's a good mother. And I'll be perfectly honest with you, I can't wait to see that precious little girl again. So I expect to see you all at the house for dinner this Sunday."

He didn't speak.

She clapped her hands together and smiled. "Now you can talk."

Sean chuckled. "Okay."

He cleared his throat and rested his arms on his desk. "I had Trent do a background check on her because she doesn't really want to talk about her ex, and I'm concerned about why."

Janean had already begun shaking her head. "The minute I give you the benefit of the doubt, you turn on me. You're just like your father and your cousins, thinking you can do anything you like just because you want something. Don't you know its an invasion of that woman's privacy to have you looking into her life before she met you?"

"Even if something in her background might be coming back to haunt her? I'm just trying to protect her."

"You're trying to control the situation, just like you

always do. Sometimes you're not going to have all the answers. You're not going to be able to fit every piece into the puzzle."

"It's not about control—it's about protection."

"Then why didn't you just ask her about this other man?"

"I did," he said, rubbing a hand over his face. "She told me they were married and they got divorced. That's all she said."

"Then that's all you need to know. For now."

He was shaking his head. "I want to know who he is and why he's not with his wife and child. I want to know what his intentions are before I—"

"Before you what? Take his place?"

He remained quiet and shrugged. Sean wasn't a hundred percent certain what he was getting ready to say— or if taking her ex's place was what he really wanted.

"Listen, if you are developing feelings for this woman, you are going to have to trust her."

"Even if I know she's holding something back?"

"That's her prerogative, son. I know you men think you are the end-all be-all because your last name is Donovan. And truth be told, I know my boys are damned good catches. But that doesn't make you indispensible. You either trust her or you'll lose her."

His mother's words resonated in his head. An hour later, he hung up with Trent without asking about the search into Tate's background. Instead he'd given his cousin all the information he had on Sabine Ravenell and Onyx Publications.

Chapter 14

"Got yourself a new car, huh, Tate? Where'd you get the money for that?"

Tate didn't even flinch when she heard his voice. After the phone call earlier, she'd known he was close. Actually, she'd spent the better part of her afternoon trying to figure out why her ex-husband would show up in Miami, of all places. He didn't love her, so she didn't believe for one moment that he'd come all this way to see her. There was a small bit of hope that he'd come to his senses and at least decided to be a part of his daughter's life. But even that she knew was too much for the selfish bastard.

"What do you want, Patrick?" she asked after she'd turned to see him standing a few feet away from where Sean's car was parked.

"Is that any way to greet your husband?" he asked, smiling as he came closer.

He'd been smiling the day she met him. In fact, Patrick was always smiling. Even the day he'd tried to explain to her why he was naked in their bed with another woman. Everything seemed to be a joke to him. He wore dark jeans and tennis shoes and an Ohio State hoodie. He liked to collect college shirts, said it was his way of donating to higher learning.

"We're divorced. Didn't you get your decree in the mail?"

He shook his head. "Must have gone to the wrong address."

"Pity," she said with a roll of her eyes. "What are you doing here?"

"Looking for you," he admitted. He reached out a hand—now that he was close enough—and touched her hair, twirling it around his finger like he used to do.

Tate pulled back. "Why?"

"I gotta tell you, Tate. I'm not feeling any love from you at the moment."

She had to laugh at that. "Whatever I felt for you disappeared the second you took that slut to my bed."

"Awww, that's in the past. Can't we move on?"

"I did. And now you're here. Can't you stay in the past?" she replied tartly and then looked over his shoulder to the elevator doors.

She'd sent Sean a text that she was on her way to the garage. His reply was that he'd meet her there. The last thing she wanted was for him to walk out and see her with Patrick. She had to get rid of him.

"Really, Patrick, what do you want? And why do you keep calling my phone and hanging up?"

"That was my mistake. Wasn't sure I had the right number."

"You're such a pathetic liar," she said with disgust building. He wasn't going to tell her why he was here and she was tired of asking.

"Just stay away from me," she told him, moving to the passenger side as if she was going to get into the car.

But she didn't have a key. She wished she did so she could get away from him. But he only followed her, grabbing her arm and pushing her up against the car.

The action set off the car's alarm, and a blaring noise filled the garage.

"You took something that belongs to me," he told her, pushing his face close to hers.

"What are you talking about?"

"When you packed up your stuff from the house, you took something of mine, and I want it back!"

He'd raised his voice, his eyes growing darker. Patrick was a darker complexion than Tate and Briana. His eyebrows were thick and usually arched to give him a sinister look. Why she hadn't noted that when she first met him, Tate had no idea. But looking at him now, feeling the bite of his fingers as he grasped her arm tightly, she felt the first tingle of fear.

"Let go of me!" she shouted, but her voice was nowhere near as loud as the car alarm. "I don't know what you're talking about!"

He opened his mouth to say something else and then was suddenly pulled away from her. Rubbing her arm, Tate righted herself just in time to see Sean's fist plowing into Patrick's jaw. Patrick stumbled backward and hit the ground. He rubbed at his face, looking up to see who had hit him.

"You bastard! You almost broke my jaw!" he yelled.

"Then get up so I can finish the job," Sean said.

It was happening so fast that Tate almost didn't have time to react. But when she saw Sean lean in to help Patrick up just so he could knock him down again, she ran forward and grabbed Sean's arm.

"No. Stop. He's not worth it," she told him.

His entire body was so rigid that when she touched him she'd almost pulled back. This was not the calm and reassuring man she'd come to know this week. It wasn't the gentle lover she'd been with last night. Fury was alive and pulsing in this man, and if she let his arm go Tate had no doubt he'd beat Patrick to near death.

"Let's just go," she said.

"Who the hell are you, and what do you want with her?" Sean asked Patrick.

By this time, Patrick had gotten to his feet, although his legs still wobbled. But he was upright and he was looking at Sean with nothing less than contempt.

"To hell with you. I don't have to answer to you!" he spat.

Sean shrugged. "Then you can answer to the police when I tell them you were not only trying to break into my car but assaulting this woman."

"It's not a big deal. Let's just go," Tate said, trying to convince Sean. She didn't want the police involved, didn't want Patrick's stay here prolonged. But her urgings were too late.

"She ain't no woman. She's my wife!" Patrick said, sounding like he was in a drunken stupor because his lower lip had already begun to swell.

Sean had left his office a few seconds after Tate had texted him, only to be stopped by Gayle with some letters that had to be signed and faxed today. The delay had allowed her to be attacked. He wasn't happy about that at all.

Regarding the bastard who'd dared to put his hands on her, Sean wasn't completely shocked. Truthfully, he could say he wasn't shocked at all. He'd known there was a reason Tate didn't want to talk about her ex, had sensed it from the beginning. Now he could see why— the guy was an ass. And apparently abusive, which won him absolutely no cool points with Sean.

"You put your hands on her again, and you're going to be her deceased husband," he told him.

Tate was holding on to his arm as if she expected him to jump over and strangle the man. Which he was really considering. Instead he used his free hand to reach into his other pocket, pull out his cell phone and quickly give their location to a 911 operator.

"You can't have me arrested for talking to my wife," the man said.

"Ex-wife, Patrick. We're not married anymore," Tate said, her voice surprisingly calm, considering how badly her hand shook on his arm and how fast her heartbeat was against his back.

"I ain't got no papers saying that. It's your word against mine," he said with a crooked smile. "Besides, I just want what she stole from me."

"I don't know what he's talking about," Tate said defensively.

She pulled on Sean's arm as she spoke and repeated it again. "I haven't even seen him in months, since I left Maryland."

It sounded as if she was trying to convince him, which was futile, since Sean didn't believe for one minute she had anything to convince him of. If she thought he believed what this man was saying, she was as crazy as her ex-husband seemed to be.

"And that's when you stole my belongings."

It was Sean's guess that in that moment, her fear turned to anger. Tate stepped away from him and fired her accusations at Patrick like she was ready to reach out and hit him herself.

"You didn't have anything else at the house, you idiot! You took everything to go and stay with your girlfriend, remember?"

Now Sean was the one to take her arm and pull her away so that she was standing behind him again.

"So, what are you—her man, now?" Patrick asked. "This is a shock. But whatever, you can have her. I just want my stuff."

Police sirens filled the area, and flashing lights and speeding vehicles came off the ramp, coming to a stop in front of them. One officer was out of the car before it even stopped.

"We got here as soon as we could, Mr. Donovan," he said to Sean. "Is this the perp?"

Sean nodded. "When I arrived he was assaulting this woman and my car alarm was going off. Ms. Denni-son's car was broken into in this same area a few days ago. Her apartment was also broken into. I think this might be your guy for all those charges."

"Right." The officer nodded.

Then his demeanor changed as he pushed Patrick around and grabbed his wrists. "Sir, you have the right to remain silent," he said, reading him his other rights.

"You just going to believe some suit over me?" Patrick yelled. "Don't I get to tell my side of the story?"

The officer's answer was to pull the handcuffs so tight that Patrick hollered once more.

"She's a thief! A lying, stupid thief!" he yelled as they pushed his head down and stuffed him into the backseat of the patrol car.

It wasn't until they pulled away that Sean finally turned to face Tate. But as he did, she started to back away from him, her head shaking, hands trembling at her side.

"Tate?" he said, taking a step closer to her.

"No," she answered in a strangled whisper. "I just have to get out of here. I have to get my baby and go."

"Okay, we'll pick up Briana and go home."

"No." She shook her head again. "Home is not with you. Home is me and Briana. That's all."

When she turned around and began to run for the elevator, all Sean could do was curse.

Chapter 15

He caught her just as the elevator doors opened and she burst inside the small compartment.

A part of her knew he would. That same part that really wanted him to.

And yet, a bigger part of her had meant what she'd said. She had no family but Briana. From the moment she'd caught Patrick in bed with that woman, then later learned who that woman was and what he'd really been doing with her—besides the obvious—she'd known they had no other alternative but to run. She'd thought Miami was far enough away. Obviously she was wrong.

The doors to the elevator closed just as Sean pressed her against the wall. He talked low, his lips right next to her ear.

"Don't run from me, Tate. I'm going to chase you wherever you go."

His voice, even in this situation, sent shivers of pleasure down her spine. Her breasts tingled and she traitorously licked her lips. Attraction should have been the last thing on her mind at that moment. And yet as he pressed close to her, it was almost all she could think about.

"I can't stay here," she whispered, closing her eyes and keeping her face to the wall. She didn't want to see him. And she didn't want him to see her.

"Why?"

"He's dangerous," was all she could bring herself to admit.

His grip loosened on her and she let her shoulders relax. The elevator wasn't moving. Sean had probably stopped it, or locked it, or something, since he seemed to be able to control anything and everything. Whereas she felt more than helpless. Again. And Tate hated that feeling.

"What did he do to you, Tate? And don't even try to say nothing."

Sean's tone was serious, but she picked up the compassion, the empathy, and she wanted to cry. Then again, she didn't. She refused. After she'd caught Patrick, and the next morning when the detectives had come to her house, she'd cried and cried for three days, nonstop. That's how she'd lost her job. On the fourth day she vowed never to shed another tear for a man, any man.

So instead, she squared her shoulders and turned so that she was now facing Sean. His warm brown eyes—the ones she was quickly becoming used to glancing into and losing all her worries—stared back at her.

"He cheated on me." It was a simple statement. One that didn't seem to shock Sean at all.

But she wasn't finished.

"With my cousin. And together they both embezzled hundreds of thousands of dollars from my grandfather."

Now he looked shocked, and Tate sighed, falling back against the wall. She crossed her arms over her chest because she didn't know what else to do with them. She didn't want to reach out and wrap her arms around Sean's neck, pull him closer and bury her head in his chest. That would feel too good to be right.

"Patrick was an investor when we first met. When I introduced him to my family, he took an instant interest in my grandfather. I didn't realize it then, but he knew an awful lot about my grandfather's work in the railroad industry and how much money he'd put away over the years after he'd invested in one of the railroad stations in Maryland.

"He asked my grandfather to let him manage his investments, but Grandpa said no. Then he and my father sat me down and warned me. Said they had a bad feeling about Patrick, that he didn't have honest eyes. That's what Grandpa said. But I was already in love by that point. I didn't believe them." She shrugged. She'd beat herself up about this for months after leaving Maryland. Now she'd resigned herself to the fact that she'd been a fool, she'd brought pain to her family and then turned her back on them in the end. It was the ultimate betrayal and the main reason why she couldn't go running to them with her baby in tow saying, "I should have listened."

"My cousin Marsha needed a job. Patrick gave her one. Then he had Marsha convince my grandfather to invest with her, but he was really investing with Patrick. I didn't find this out until after I found Patrick and Marsha in my bed. Detectives came to my house the very next morning. It seems Patrick dumped Marsha for some other mistress and she ran straight to the police with everything she knew. My grandfather lost his entire life's savings."

Sean had lifted a palm to her cheek. Tate couldn't resist, and she leaned into his touch. Accepting his comfort was one thing. Leaning on him completely was another. She couldn't make that type of mistake again. But then he wrapped his other arm around her waist and pulled her to him.

"It's not your fault. None of it is your fault," he assured her.

And some part of Tate knew his words were true. How could she have known Patrick was a liar, a cheater and a thief? There were signs like the ones she wrote about in her column every day, but in the beginning he'd been perfect, attentive, loving, respectful. She knew now it had all been an act. One that she'd bought completely and that had ultimately cost her everything.

"I did what I warn women not to do every day. I trusted him with everything I had, everything that was precious to me. And he used that. He used me to get what he wanted. Then he left. He walked right out the door without ever looking back. He hasn't seen Briana in almost a year, and he doesn't care."

"That's his loss," Sean said tightly. "He's the asshole here, not you. And Briana's much better off without scum like him in her life."

She was nodding her head, because she actually did

believe what he was saying. None of it kept her from feeling like hell, but she believed him.

"What does he think you stole from him?"

He was holding her now, and her head had fallen right onto his chest just the way she'd imagined it would. And it felt oh so good, until he'd asked her that question. She raised her head to look at him.

"I honestly don't know what he's talking about. He took stuff out of our house that night and he never came back. I thought he had everything he wanted. I had movers come in and pack everything else a month later when I moved out."

Sean was nodding as she spoke.

"Do you really think he was the one who broke into my house and my car?" she asked incredulously.

"Yes. I think he was."

She lowered her head again, feeling the "stupid" stamp on her forehead once more. The feel of Sean's finger lifting her chin in that way he did washed it completely away.

"I'm not going to let him get near you again. Don't you worry about that or about Briana. I'm going to take care of you both."

"Why?" she heard herself asking. "You barely know me. I'm your employee, and I'm bringing all of this unwanted baggage into your life."

He didn't answer with words but touched her lips softly with his own. As it was with them, the kiss quickly grew urgent, his arms wrapping around her as he held her tightly against him.

Tate draped her arms around his neck, pulling him closer. She loved holding him like this, loved feeling his strength surrounding her. Kissing him was an added bonus as his tongue stroked hers in what she could only describe as a loving manner. But Tate was a realist, and she didn't believe in love at first sight. And she definitely didn't believe a man like Sean Donovan would fall in love with a single mother in just a couple of days. Life did not work that way—especially not hers.

Sean couldn't let her go. Sure, they were in an elevator that would probably override the locked command he'd hit and begin moving any minute now. But even that didn't seem to matter.

All he knew was that she was in his arms. This woman that he'd just met but already couldn't imagine his days without. From her dimpled smile to her quick wit and candid personality, he couldn't seem to get enough of her.

His hands slid down from her back to her waist, where his fingers flared outward over her buttocks. She gasped and he licked along the line of her lips. He was hard and ready to take her. She pressed against him, and he knew he'd get no argument from her. But they were in an elevator, he reminded himself. Tate deserved much better than this.

"We should get going," he said, his lips still close to hers.

She nodded but didn't release the hold she had on his neck.

"I love kissing you," he willingly admitted.

A smile touched her lips a second before she gave them to him again.

She pulled away slowly and said, "I love kissing you, too."

Of course that warranted another kiss, and he pressed

even closer to her, pushing her legs apart and grabbing one thigh with the intent of lifting it and wrapping her leg around his waist. But that was too much. He had to stop. Breathing heavily, he tore his mouth away from hers but rested his forehead on hers and sighed. "We have to pick up Briana."

She nodded. "Right."

With every ounce of strength he could muster, Sean turned away from Tate and pushed the button to activate the elevator. The doors opened on the garage floor they'd been on all along, and he stepped out into the late afternoon breeze. Tate followed and he took her hand.

"We'll probably have to give the police a report. You up for that?" he asked as they walked to the car.

"Yes. But I still don't know what he could be looking for," she admitted.

"Doesn't matter," Sean told her after he'd helped her into the passenger seat. "Like I said, it's his loss."

He kissed her forehead before closing her in the car. As he walked around to the other side, he pulled out his cell phone and sent Trent a text. He wanted his cousin to know he now had another name for him to investigate, and he wanted that information back ASAP.

Chapter 16

Tate sat on the terrace, her legs stretched out in a lounge chair with Briana in her lap. They'd had dinner and Briana had splashed enough water around in the bathroom to make someone believe they had four or five kids in this condo. Briana was winding down, her little eyes drowsy as she lay against Tate's chest, breathing steadily.

Sean had told her he had some business phone calls to make, so he'd closed himself in the office he kept on the first floor just off the living room. She'd walked the entire length of this condo, looking inside every room, deciding on the least conspicuous places to store her and Briana's belongings. The last thing she wanted was to be in Sean's way, even though he insisted they were no trouble.

She was starting to believe him when he said that,

because their dinners together went along so seamlessly it was almost as if they'd been together for years. Tonight Tate had decided to cook, even though they still had leftover spaghetti. She was a stickler for not wasting food, so she'd made note to carry that for lunch tomorrow. Tonight she'd cooked fried chicken, steamed broccoli and scalloped potatoes. Briana had played happily with her chicken bone after eating the meat from the drumstick, and Sean had complimented her on the crispy chicken. It had been her mother's recipe, so she was proud to accept the compliment.

It had been perfect. Almost too perfect, she thought.

And she loved this view. The Miami skyline at dusk was absolutely beautiful. The light breeze helped to lull Briana to sleep, and if Tate weren't careful, she might find herself drifting soon as well.

"You look nice and relaxed."

His voice startled her because she hadn't heard him approach. But now Sean was sitting on the edge of the corner lounge chair, leaning forward with his elbows on his knees.

"Actually, I think I was dozing off," she admitted with a lazy grin.

"She was tired tonight," he said with a nod toward Briana.

Tate looked down at her daughter. "Yeah, Ellen at day care said she had a ball at the playground this afternoon."

"She's happy and healthy and beautiful, just like her mother."

As always, his voice sounded honest and sincere.

"Do you want children?" she asked him abruptly. "I

mean, one day, eventually, do you want to have kids of your own?"

His arm had already extended by the time she finished her question. Long, strong fingers rubbed softly over Briana's cheek, ruffled her hair and then touched the small gold bead in her earlobe.

"I come from a really big family, and we all stick close together. There's never been any doubt in my mind that I'd one day start my own family." He looked back up at her and smiled, pulling his hand slowly away from Briana. "I guess that means yes, I'd like to have kids."

That statement was like a ray of sunshine on a cloudy day. Tate wanted more children, always had.

"When I was a little girl, I used to daydream about having this big country wedding. My grandfather's house is near the Eastern Shore and sits on a piece of land right by the water. I wanted to get married outside and then move into a big house just like the one I grew up in. I wanted lots of children and to sit on my back porch and write." She stopped when she felt like she was sharing too much.

He looked at her like he was waiting for her to continue. So she did.

"I married Patrick at the courthouse because he didn't want all the fanfare of a big wedding. My family didn't like him and he didn't really care for them, so I saw them less and less as we lived and worked in the city. I haven't seen them for two whole years. They've never even met Briana."

This time she stopped because she was afraid her next words would get lost in the lump of emotion clogged in her throat. Absentmindedly she rubbed Briana's hair and looked away, toward the starless sky.

"I never imagined what my wedding would be like or what type of house I'd live in," Sean began.

His voice was like a calming switch that she liked activating.

"I just knew that I wanted my life to be just like my parents' lives. They have a happy marriage, though not without disagreements—because let me tell you, if Janean Donovan doesn't get her way, whew! My dad's great at dealing with her though. I think it's because of how deep their love for one another is. We always had people around—family, cousins and uncles—and our family reunions were fantastic."

"Family is so important," she admitted. "I forgot that for a while."

"You should call them," he said. "I'll bet they're worried and concerned."

She nodded. "My oldest sister, Blake, she used to email me. But I guess she got tired of not getting an answer. And my other sister, Jamie, stopped trying, too. After a while I just didn't know what to say."

"But you know what to say to everyone else. Maybe you should write a letter to 'Ask Jenny' and get some advice. I hear Jenny's smart as hell and shoots straight from the hip."

Tate smiled, her eyes finding his once more. "You fix everything, don't you? You find the problem and make it better. I'll bet you've been doing that all your life."

"Actually, my brother tells me I worry things to death." He laughed, a full-bodied sound that cocooned them both. "Then I fix the problem."

"See, I knew it."

Their laughter died down, but the layer of comfort stayed with them.

"You're good at it," she told him.

He shrugged. "Only when it really counts."

"And does this really count? I mean, I keep telling myself not to overthink this, not to make too much out of it. But I just have to ask, is this real? Sean Donovan, of *Infinity* magazine and the world-renowned Donovans, with me?" She knew she had said it as if she considered herself nothing, or beneath him in some way. But that wasn't how she meant it. She just never imagined herself with a man like Sean before. Not a rich man, or an important businessman, but a good man who had the sense to recognize a good woman even through the shield.

He stood without a word and leaned down to take Briana from her arms. "Stay right there," he told her.

She took in the sight of him cradling her daughter in his arms and looking down at her as if she were the stars in the sky. She knew the image would be forever emblazoned in her mind. Minutes later he was back, and he'd left Briana in her crib.

He held two glasses of wine. He handed her one and then scooted her to the side so he could sit on the same lounge chair she was on.

"Take a sip," he told her.

She did and watched as he did the same.

"Sweet?" he asked.

She nodded. "Very, but soft, too. I like it."

"So do I."

He took a deep breath. "Smell that?"

She inhaled and exhaled. "Springtime, flowers, life."

He nodded. Then Sean touched a finger to her lower lip. Tate trembled.

"Feel that?"

"Yes," she whispered.

"Where do you feel it, and how does it make you feel?"

He dipped his finger into the glass of wine and then touched it to her lips again. She couldn't help it—her tongue extended, and she licked the tip of his finger.

"Every time you touch me, Sean, I feel it all over. It's sweet and it's fresh and new."

"Like the wine and the air and me sitting here with you. It's real, Tate. You, this beautiful woman who fell right into my life like fate had brought you here just for me. And me, a man who seemingly has everything but was looking for so much more. We are real."

He'd been moving closer, and now his face was just inches from hers.

She nodded. "It's real?"

His lips brushed over hers. "You bet your pretty ass it's real."

The desire he had for her was just as real. It was real and it was potent.

Sean placed his glass on the floor. When he turned back to her, she was drinking hers again, licking tiny droplets from her lips when she finished. He circled his fingers around her wrist and removed the glass from her hand. She was watching him closely, waiting with the barest amount of restraint.

She'd changed out of the skirt and blouse she'd worn to work and now wore shorts and a tank top. He traced along the rim of the top and along the hill of her breasts. She sucked in a breath when he palmed both globes. He watched her face as his hands worked over her breasts. Her eyes were half closed, her mouth slightly open as she struggled to breathe regularly. She'd pulled her hair back into a messy bun with several wisps pulling free, which tickled her face as her head swayed from side to side.

On impulse, he pulled the shirt over her head, loving that her breasts were unbound and out for him to see freely. They were heavy in his hands, a natural feel that he loved so much more than the store-bought breasts women preferred nowadays. Her turgid nipples rolled over the palm of his hands, poked through his fingers. Sean heard his own gasp as his erection hardened significantly. He wore basketball shorts and a T-shirt, so there was no hiding his desire.

When she grabbed his wrists, pushing his hands down her torso, he almost groaned. Almost.

Instead, he pushed her shorts down her legs and off, using his fingers to pull the band of her panties down. She was gloriously naked now, lying back on the lounge chair like a *Playboy* model. Suddenly Sean wanted nothing more than to snap a mental picture of her, just like this, and keep it in his mind for all time.

"Your turn," she whispered, one finger tracing along her lower lip.

She didn't have to ask him twice. Sean stood, quickly pushing his shorts and boxers down and stepping out of them. He pulled his shirt off so fast he could have sworn he heard the cotton rip.

This time when he lowered himself to the lounge he pushed her legs open so that they dangled off each side and she was spread before him like a delectable feast. He touched her there, right in the center, letting his fingers part her moistened folds. She sighed with his touch, and when he looked up at her, he was pleased to see her licking her lips and watching him closely.

"You are simply beautiful," he told her.

"Only for you," she said.

He leaned forward, the fingers of one hand still exploring her center. His lips touched hers. "Always," he whispered over her lips. "Always."

Her tongue greeted his with a loving swipe, and Sean sank deeper, his tongue in her mouth, two fingers pushing gently into her opening. She bucked beneath him, her teeth nipping his lip as she moaned. He pumped his fingers inside her while the tip of his erection wept with arousal. A light breeze tickled his bare skin, but Sean barely noticed as he pulled both his lips and fingers away from her.

Pushing at her thighs, he buried his face between her legs and licked along her plump folds. Her nails pinched at his shoulders as she gripped him tight, thrusting upward to meet his touch. She was intoxicating, her scent, her flavor—everything about her made Sean drunk with desire. As his tongue found the tightened bud, he lapped at it hungrily, loving the stiff feel of her in his mouth.

"Sean!" she yelled as her entire body trembled.

He held her right there, his hands tight on her hips as he continued his brutally erotic assault. Her release was sweet, the sound of his name in her voice melodic. He wanted to yell it to the world, the second he felt himself sinking, drowning, falling in love with Tate Dennison.

Every ounce of her body had been engulfed in a torrential heat storm orchestrated by Sean's mouth. She'd known it was a dangerous instrument that he wielded with the greatest skill, since his kisses were so seductive and addictive. It was no wonder those kisses applied to her most vulnerable of parts would prove deadly. Her thighs still trembled, even as his tongue traced adoring paths up and down the insides.

Tate wanted to scream again, but she feared someone might hear her since they were outside. Sean's condo was a penthouse, but she didn't want to take any chances. What she did want was to return the favor.

The way he looked at her, talked to her, said her name, touched her body, all of it had emboldened her. Tate pushed up from the lounge, moving her hands from Sean's shoulders to his biceps as he looked up at her. She stood and he followed her over to the sectional seats. When he moved to take her in his arms, she resisted, touching her lips to his chest, stroking her tongue over his pectorals. He held the back of her head gently with one hand, the other stroking her bare arm.

"Tate," he whispered, and she shivered. "You drive me crazy. Your body, your smile, your touch."

His words made her float. She loved the intimacy they shared, the closeness she'd never experienced before.

"I love touching you," she admitted, letting her fingers fan over his torso, down to his rock-solid abs, over his sculpted hips.

"Touch all you want," he encouraged.

She took his advice, lowering herself until she was sitting on the seat, with her palms grasping his muscled buttocks. He shifted with her, moving to stand between her legs, his fingers buried in her hair.

She pulled back and stared at his length. He was long and hard, the tip of his erection arrowed directly at her. She glimpsed the tiny bead of arousal, and her mouth watered. Of their own accord, her fingers drifted until they were wrapped around his thickness. She rubbed tentatively at the base of his shaft and was rewarded by a deep groan and a tightening of his grip on her hair. This was all new to Tate, so she was operating purely on instinct. And right now instinct told her to continue.

She stroked her hands upward to the bulbous tip. He sucked in a breath and that bead of arousal grew larger. She couldn't stop herself if she wanted to. Tate dipped her head, touched her tongue to his tip and let the moistness linger there.

"Baby." It was a strangled cry from his lips. A tone to his voice she'd never heard before.

Tate took that as a good sign, lavishing his tip with her tongue, showing him just how much she desired him. Sean held on to her, guiding her head with his soft strokes until neither of them could wait another moment.

He pulled away from her, pushing her back on the chair and lifting her legs so that they draped over his shoulders. He entered her in one long, hard stroke that left Tate completely breathless. He thrust deep, pulled out completely and then sank back inside of her. Her mouth opened, breath gushing out as she tried to hold on for the tumultuous ride.

Tate was swept away, not just in lust or desire but in the magical wonder of falling in love. She'd read about it in romance novels, heard about it from high school friends and craved it for the better part of her life. But in this moment, as Sean continued to work slowly and methodically in and out of her, as her body welcomed him completely, she knew this was the first time ever that she'd felt it for herself.

He shifted again, releasing her legs and turning them

so that she lay on her back, her entire body on the chair, his on top of hers. His thickness still filled her, the proximity causing an erotic friction that made her eyes close.

"Tate," he said, but it wasn't a whisper. It was a command.

She opened her eyes, found him glaring down at her, his lips parted, brows furrowed. Tate lifted her hands to cup his face in her palms.

"I've never felt this way before. You make me feel so good," she told him honestly. It was easy with him to just open her mouth and let the words come out. She wasn't embarrassed or self-conscious at all.

"Baby." He lowered his forehead to hers and continued to move in and out of her.

"Yes, Sean, yes!" she moaned, loving the feel of him all over.

Their release came simultaneously, an eruption that rocked them hard enough to have them gasping for breath and almost falling off the seat. He wrapped his arms around her so tightly and held her so close that Tate almost couldn't breathe.

"I love you."

It was muffled, said with his face buried in the crook of her neck. But she heard it. Her mind hit instant replay and she heard it again and again. No, she realized, he was actually saying it. Over and over and over, he was telling her he loved her.

And tears filled her eyes.

Chapter 17

"They were married just over three years ago, and the divorce was finalized earlier this year. He was charged federally last year with fraud, but they haven't gone to trial yet. He made a half-million-dollar bail, and there are no offshore accounts in his name," Trent reported via conference call early Saturday morning.

Sean was in his office once more. He'd left a sleeping and very tempting Tate still naked in bed. This phone call was damned important.

"Where's he getting his money now?" he asked.

"That's a good question. Tate was never charged. She had a savings account when they divorced. Smart girl. Used it to relocate to Miami, where she now resides. Her credit's good, she barely buys anything that doesn't look like a necessity. Pays for day care, car payment. That's it."

"He says she took something from him. Was real adamant about it. I'm thinking it has to be money. He seems like the kind of guy to be driven by dollar signs."

Trent cleared his throat. "I agree. But I don't know what it could be. My buddy Devlin Bonner is in the area between government assignments. I've already given him your address, told him to stick to you and Tate like glue. He should be there by noon today."

"I don't need a bodyguard," Sean said gruffly. If Patrick Dennison was released from jail and made any attempt to get near Tate again, he planned to finish the ass-kicking he'd started yesterday.

"Until I get a lock on who this dude might be working with, you both get a guard. He's not working alone, Sean, that's for sure. And if he's got Feds on his ass, he could be real dangerous. Just do me a favor and go along for the time being."

He didn't like it, but Sean heard what Trent was saying. His cousin was an ex–Navy SEAL, which meant his friend Devlin probably was as well. If Trent thought he warranted sending this guy to be with them, he'd go along, for Tate's sake.

"You get anything on Ravenell?" he asked, switching the subject.

"She's another elusive one. I did find a couple of accounts. She's sitting on about four million liquid. Her business accounts aren't looking as heavy."

"But her sales are steady."

"Yeah, but not near as steady as *Infinity*'s. You've got the name and all its connections behind you. Company stock is high and rising. She doesn't look as stable. The money in her personal account she has is new, too— about eight to nine months ago there was a big deposit.

It looks like it's from a dummy business. I have to dig a little further to get that info."

Sean nodded, drumming his fingers over the desk. He was leaning back in his chair, staring out the window as he listened to Trent.

"So if we accepted her offer, how is she planning to come up with the money to buy *Infinity?*"

"Don't know. If she took out a loan she wouldn't stay afloat long. She'd have to get investors to keep it going. But I know you aren't considering that."

"Of course not. Besides, the decision to sell wouldn't be my decision alone. Dad would never go for it, neither would Uncle Reggie. No, I just want to make sure I know what our position is."

"You want all your ducks in a row before you plow her ass," Trent said with a chuckle.

"You know it," Sean said. "I'm going to set up a meeting to get this over with once and for all."

"Good idea. Take reinforcements," Trent warned.

Sean frowned. "To meet with Sabine? She's not dangerous, just a little out of touch."

"She's making this insane offer to buy the magazine, and she's connected to some pretty unsavory characters. Do what I say and take someone with you. Take Savian—his serious ass would scare anybody away."

Sean laughed and felt a little of his stress melt away. "Savian's getting better."

"You still don't lie good, man. I talked to Parker last week, and he said his brother was in dire need of some lovin'."

"If I know Parker, he didn't put it that delicately."

"Of course not. Said something about getting that monkey off Savian's back."

The cousins laughed and talked a little about the up-coming reunion that was being planned. The Donovans, the entire clan, tried to get together at least once a year. This year the suggestion was for them to visit the private island they owned in the Caribbean.

After hanging up the phone, Sean sat thinking about Briana on the white sand beaches, taking her to play in the clear blue water, sharing the sights of the island with Tate. He thought about them doing lots of things together. In fact, all he could do was think about the three of them as some sort of unit now, a family.

"I'm nervous," Tate admitted when they stepped up to the door at the Big House.

"You've been here before," Sean said, adjusting Briana on his hip and reaching for the doorknob.

"But that was before." She didn't want to verbalize what she meant by "before," but she raised her eyebrows at him and was graced with his full laughter once more. It seemed like they'd been laughing and enjoying each other all weekend.

"Before we had sex. I get it. But I promise you I won't bring that up," he told her and opened the door.

They stepped into the foyer, which Tate remembered from before. She looked over the shining champagne-and-gold marbled floor and the thick winding banister that accompanied wide steps. There was artwork on the walls and huge potted plants on either side of the arch-way that led to the main living room. It was huge and stately and homely all at once.

The minute they entered, Lyra came in from the living room. "Finally," she said with a warm smile as she walked over to take Briana from Sean's arms. "Hi,

Tate. Come on in here with the womenfolk," she said, nodding toward the living room.

Tate looked to Sean, who was smiling and nodding at her. Elbowing him in the ribs probably wouldn't go over too well at this moment, but she promised she'd pay him back later. Instead she followed behind Lyra, who was dressed in a long sundress and high-heeled sandals. Her hair was pulled away from her face and held in place with a headband.

Tate had opted for a sundress as well, in a pale yellow color and a few inches shorter than Lyra's. Its filmy material circled around her calves. Her white bolero jacket capped her shoulders and made her full breasts look a little smaller. Her sandals weren't as high as Lyra's—only two-and-a-half-inch heels. She'd dressed Briana in yellow as well. Bright yellow shorts and a tank top with eyelet trim. Her cap was all-white eyelet, and her sandals where white with butterfly clasps.

Her daughter smiled happily at Lyra and drank up every word the woman said like it was formula. When Lyra sat down and lowered Briana to the floor, Tate was shocked to see her daughter walk right over to a particular table and pull at a seashell that was sitting there. Instinctively she jumped up to get it from her, not knowing how expensive the piece may be.

"Oh, let her go. It's nothing that can't be replaced."

Tate turned at the sound of the mature female voice and smiled nervously when she recognized that it was Janean Donovan, Sean's mother.

She looked just as attractive as when Tate had met her a few days ago. Her tan slacks were perfectly pressed, and the cream-colored V-neck tunic comple-mented her full figure well. Brown curls framed a full face with high cheekbones and a sprinkle of brown freckles across the bridge of her nose. Her smile was friendly, her eyes welcoming, and still Tate's heart beat like she'd just run a marathon.

"Hi again, Mrs. Donovan," Tate said. Janean moved closer to take Tate's outstretched hand in both of hers.

"Hello, Tate. I hear you've been going through a lot lately. Here, sit down and relax."

Tate took the seat. It was a large chair and looked as if it should fit more than one person. Tate sat back, taking slow breaths. "There has been a lot going on."

"Including you sleeping with my cousin," Regan said as she made her way into the room and sat on the couch next to Lyra.

Tate gulped.

"Iced tea?" asked another female who looked to be the same age as Mrs. Donovan.

Tate gratefully took the glass from the other woman.

"I'm Carolyn Donovan, married to Reginald. You must forgive my daughter, Regan. She's never been able to hold her tongue."

"What? I just said what we're all thinking," Regan said with her eyes still on Tate.

It wasn't a mean glare, Tate surmised. She'd been on the receiving end of a mean female glare before, and this wasn't it. But Regan was definitely curious. She wanted to know what Tate's intentions were, wanted to make sure Tate wasn't just trying to take advantage of Sean and the Donovans. She could relate to that.

So she smiled at Carolyn, who wore a long sage-green skirt and matching blouse. Her skin was like milk chocolate, and her eyes were a lovely almond shape. Regan looked a lot like her mother.

"It's all right, Mrs. Donovan," she said. "I completely understand and appreciate Regan's candor." Tate took a sip of her tea and then cleared her throat.

"For the record, yes, Sean and I are sleeping together. We haven't been for very long, but I'm pleased with the direction our relationship has taken." That was the first time she'd admitted that aloud. It felt good.

Lyra chuckled. "Well, I guess that answers your questions," she told Regan.

Tate shook her head. "No, but I have an answer for that as well. I'm not rich. I was married before and now I'm divorced. I love and need my job at *Infinity* but not enough to sleep with the boss to get ahead. What Sean and I have is separate from work, and we'll most likely keep it that way."

There, she'd set them all straight. She hoped.

"Well, now *that* answered my question," Janean said. "And for the record, my question wasn't if you were trying to use my son. Sean's a smart boy, probably the smartest of this whole bunch here. He would know if a woman was using him, and he'd put her quickly in her place. So if he's bringing you and your daughter to us, that means something. And you just confirmed that you're feeling the same way about him. I'd say that's cause for celebration. Dinner will be ready in five minutes."

And with that Janean and Carolyn both left the room.

"We're not normally like this," Lyra told Tate when Tate was looking like she didn't know what to say or do next.

To keep her calm, she watched Briana waddle around the room, smacking her small hands on the tables and basically exploring every inch of this large room. On the one side there were floor-to-ceiling doors that looked out to a deck and a sprawling lawn. Briana would love to get out there and play. Thankfully the doors were closed.

"I can see why you'd feel protective of him. There's a lot at stake."

Regan shook her head. "No, it's nothing like that. I mean, it's not just about the money. As far as I can remember, no Donovan man has given his money to an unworthy woman. We're more concerned about Sean being hurt in any way."

"I would never hurt him," Tate said adamantly.

"But your circumstances could," Regan replied.

She nodded. "You're right. But I didn't ask him to get involved. I don't even know what Patrick wants. He just showed up."

"Patrick is your ex-husband?" Lyra asked.

"Yes. I haven't seen him in almost a year, and he just showed up here yesterday. I don't know why."

Regan crossed her long legs, the short ivory skirt she wore giving way. "Maybe he found out you were dating a Donovan."

"Then why not just ask me or Sean for money? Why break into my car and into my house?" Tate wondered.

"She's right," Lyra said, going to the door to play with Briana, who was tapping on the glass.

"Exes are idiots, no matter what. You should write that in your column."

Tate had to laugh at Regan. The woman looked absolutely serious as she spoke.

"Exes and guys who think they're walking gods

when they're actually living breathing asses," Regan continued.

"Ah, okay. I'll take that into consideration." Tate didn't know what else to say to that.

"She's not talking about your ex now," Lyra said as she came back to her seat with a clapping Briana in tow. "She's talking about Gavin Lucas, a man she despises."

"I don't despise him. I hate everything about him, from his spit-shined Jimmy Choo loafers to that stupid mole on his left jaw. He's everything I hate about a man."

Regan's tirade was interesting. Tate couldn't help but respond, "And everything you love about them."

"What?" Regan asked in a tone that said she didn't want to hear what Tate was about to say.

Well, Tate hadn't wanted to be questioned like she was at an inquisition either, but that hadn't stopped Ms. Regan Donovan from doing so.

"You love a somewhat arrogant man. One who's confident and sure of himself and everything that he does. To be up to your standards he'd have to give as well as he could take. You say you hate him, and I'll bet if he was here he'd say the same to you. Two very dominant and assertive creatures are bound to butt heads, but they're also almost certain to fall hard when the love bug bites. Their connection would be fierce and stronger than either of their personalities alone. So yeah, he's everything you love about a man." She shrugged. "Unfortunately."

Lyra chuckled. "You are absolutely perfect for Sean!"

Regan seethed for a second and then lifted her own glass and took a sip. "Yes, I agree. She's absolutely perfect for my cousin."

* * *

Dinner was fabulous. Tate hadn't enjoyed a home-cooked meal like it in ages. They were enjoying coffee and dessert on the deck, with the ladies in lounge chairs and the men standing near the bar. Briana had fallen asleep and was content in the portable crib that Janean had mysteriously pulled out of one of the closets. She'd said it was left over from one of her children, but Tate knew that wasn't true. Her children were both grown men, and this box with the crib in it still had a tag on it with a delivery date of two days ago.

Tate had been warmed by the idea that Mrs. Donovan was preparing for Briana to spend time at her house. Briana had never had a grandmother, and she could do worse than Janean Donovan.

The conversation had turned to their upcoming family reunion, and Tate was listening with only half an ear. She missed her own family terribly. She thought about what Sean had said and considered calling, or at the very least emailing, her sister Blake.

When Tate thought nothing could disturb this quiet family-filled evening, flashing lights invaded the darkness.

"We've got company," Dion said, walking past the women toward the front of the house.

"And not the welcome kind," Savian said with a frown.

Tate was already standing when she felt Sean's hand on her shoulder. "Stay here," he told her.

Sean gave his cousin a nod, and Regan came to stand beside Tate. "We'll just wait until we see what's going on," Regan told her.

Out of the shadows of the night, a man who looked

like one of those wrestlers on TV came sauntering over to her. "Stay close to me, Ms. Dennison."

"Who are you?" Regan asked.

Tate wanted to know the answer to that question, too, but unfortunately the unwanted guests had arrived.

"Good evening," said one of the policemen who had walked out to the deck. "We're here to take Sean Donovan and Tate Dennison in for questioning. Right now, no one is under arrest, so we'd appreciate your cooperation."

This came from an officer with one hand on his belt and the other gripping a long stick. Two more officers were behind him.

"What the hell are you talking about? This is my home," Bruce Donovan said. "And just what do you want with my son and his girlfriend?"

"Your son has been accused of assault. We'd like to ask him a few questions about that. Ms. Dennison has been accused of theft, and we need to get to the bottom of that."

"Patrick," Tate whispered and made a move toward the police. She wanted to tell them that Patrick was a thieving liar, but the bulky man stopped her.

"We'll go to the station," Sean said finally.

He moved around Dion, who'd stood in front of him, and then came to stand beside Tate, taking her hand. When he looked up and nodded at the large man, Tate presumed they knew each other.

"I'll drive them," the man said.

"Who the hell are you?" Regan asked again.

"Devlin Bonner. Trent sent me," he said in a voice deeper and raspier than any Tate had ever heard.

She didn't know who Trent was, but she assumed

the rest of the family did, because they all breathed a collective sigh.

"Briana…" Tate started to say.

"I'll keep an eye on her, don't you worry. And you'll be back shortly to pick her up," Janean said with absolute certainty.

Tate wasn't so sure. She'd never been taken to a police station before.

Chapter 18

The room was cool, with drab gray walls, a table and two chairs. In front of her there was a cup of coffee that looked more like crude oil. In her lap were her hands, no longer shaking but a little sweaty. Her back was straight and her mind focused on telling the truth.

"Tate Dennison?" A woman dressed in what almost looked like a three-piece suit said in a crisp tone.

"Yes," she answered, determined to look the woman right in the eye. She wasn't going to be intimidated, wasn't going to back down, because she knew she had done nothing wrong.

"And you were married to Patrick Dennison?"

She'd taken a seat across from Tate, opening a folder and reading the first sheet of paper there.

"Yes. We were divorced a year ago."

"And you two have a daughter together?"

Tate nodded. "My daughter is two years old."

"When was the last time you saw your ex-husband?"

Tate had been over this in her head a million times. "Before this recent incident, it was April third, two days before our divorce was final."

"And did you talk to him then?"

Tate nodded.

"What did you talk about?"

"He wanted to make sure I wasn't going to change my mind about child support. I gave it up for a quick dissolution of the marriage."

The officer looked at her then, with a shocked expression on her face. After a few moments she shook her head and went back to the papers in the file.

"He says you stole something from him, but he won't say what it is. Do you have any idea what he's talking about?"

Tate shook her head. "I absolutely do not. And believe me, I've been thinking about it a lot since seeing Patrick yesterday. If I had something of his, I'd give it back to him so fast he wouldn't know what hit him. Whatever it takes to get him out of my life for good."

"So if you had something of his, you'd give it back?"

"Damn right I would. And for the record, he's the one who broke into my car and stole my daughter's car seat. He also broke into my house. Then he physically assaulted me in the parking garage. I should be pressing charges against *him*."

The detective straightened her papers and closed her file. She flattened her palms on the table and looked directly at Tate. "You're absolutely right. You should be pressing charges against him. I'd highly advise you to do so. And another thing—get your child support or get him to give up his rights to your child."

Tate was stunned. She let her own hands fall to the tabletop and blinked a few times trying to decide if she'd heard correctly.

"Boy, you don't beat around the bush, do you?" she asked with a slight chuckle. Her chest was heaving with relief.

"No," she said with a smile. "I don't. He's an ass. Want him out of your life for good? Get him out of your daughter's life. Believe me, I've dealt with more than my share of deadbeat dad drama. If he doesn't want any part of your child, then put him out of her life totally."

She was standing now, and for the first time Tate recognized the signs. This woman was probably in her mid-thirties. She had children but no wedding ring. She looked tired, most likely worked long hours and then spent even more hours with her kids at home because she, too, was a single parent. Her advice had been startlingly clear, and, as one who made her living giving advice, Tate thought she should at least take it into consideration.

She stood, too, wiping her hands over her skirt as she did. She extended her hand to the officer and smiled. "Thank you."

The officer nodded and offered her hand. "Detective Linds. It was nice to meet you, ma'am."

"Same here," Tate said.

And when the detective was gone she sat back down, let her head fall into her hands and sighed again.

"Sounds like self-defense to me," Devlin said once Sean had gone through his account of the events.

Devlin wasn't an attorney and by no means should have been allowed in the interrogation room with Sean and the two detectives. But Sean was a Donovan. His father played golf with the mayor, and his mother served on a committee alongside the governor's wife. It was apparent that the police department had been warned to allow him some liberties.

Only mildly agitated by the fact that he'd been brought here at all, Sean really just wanted to get back to Tate as soon as possible.

"But he didn't assault you first," Detective Alvarez said to Sean with an even glare.

Sean shook his head. "He did not. He did, however, have Ms. Dennison in a tight grip and had pushed her against the car. I had reason to fear for her life."

Detective Sessom, a thirty-something African American female, gave him an understanding look. "I think that'll be all for now."

Alvarez, the fiftyish male, smirked. "Yeah, don't leave town."

Sean stood. "I wouldn't think of it."

"What about Dennison?" Devlin asked.

"He's trying to make bail. That's why he keeps yelling about Ms. Dennison having something that belongs to him. I get the impression it's something expensive, something that can be sold to make his bond," Sessom replied.

Sean shook his head as he and Devlin moved toward the door. "You might want to check with the Feds before you let him go. I hear he's got their attention for fraud."

Alvarez stepped his burly body in front of Sean and asked, "And how do you know this?"

Devlin stepped closer, as if he were trying to wedge

his own muscular body between Alvarez and Sean. "We have our sources looking into this as well. So take the tip and contact the Feds about your prisoner before you let him walk."

Sean walked out of the room with Devlin right behind him. At the same time a door across the hall opened and he saw Tate standing there. He went to her immediately, pulling her into his arms when he was close enough.

"He's in jail, and he's going to stay there. I don't want you to worry," he told her.

He was stunned when she pulled back and looked up at him. "I'm not worried. I just want to get Briana and go home."

Home was his place, Sean realized after her words had a few seconds to sink in. She would never return to that apartment if he had anything to do with it.

In the early morning hours, Tate rolled over in search of the man who had been holding her throughout the night. She'd had a bad dream, as juvenile as that sounded, and she instantly reached for his comfort.

But Sean wasn't there.

Panic hit her like a sucker punch to the gut, and she bolted out of bed. Her bare feet slapped across the hardwood floors leading to the guest room they'd temporarily made into Briana's nursery. The crib that Sean had purchased yesterday sat at an angle so that when Briana awoke she could look up through the floor-to-ceiling windows and see either the sun or the moon. Sean thought that was better than a mobile and swore Briana liked the outside scenery best. Tate hadn't argued because, well, Briana hadn't argued. So Sean must have been right.

Only this time, Briana wasn't in the crib.

Panic soared through Tate like a spreading fire. She clutched at her throat as air struggled to make it through from her lungs. She took the stairs two at a time, almost falling down the last couple but holding onto the railing for dear life. She came to a quick stop when she saw through the living room that the patio doors were open.

Heart still tapping a quick, rhythmic beat in her chest, she walked to the door before stopping to stand completely still. She stared.

Sean walked back and forth, his steps slow and measured. Briana lay on his shoulder, her wide eyes staring right at him. His feet were bare, shorts hanging attractively at his hips, chest also bare. He supported her by her bottom, his other hand with a finger that Briana held tightly. As he walked he talked in a hushed tone to Briana.

Tate couldn't hear what he was saying, but whatever it was, Briana was mesmerized. For endless moments Tate stood there, arms folded across her chest, watching this man with her daughter. Every so often he'd dip his head and kiss her forehead. Briana's chubby cheeks would rise with a smile. Then Sean would smile, looking at her as if he'd never seen anything that precious before.

She knew that look and knew the feeling that went along with it. Sometimes she'd simply hold Briana in her arms and look at her that way. Inside she'd be filled with an unconditional love that was all encompassing. Tears blurred her eyes as she wondered if Sean were feeling that same way. Then, because her feet refused to stay still a moment longer, she walked toward them. When he saw her he stopped and turned to face her. Then, to her further astonishment, he released the hand holding Briana's and extended his arm to her. Tate walked into his embrace willingly. Then they stood, the three of them swaying in the slight breeze, as if there were some music around that only they could hear.

Concentration came even easier this morning as Sean sat at his desk poring over sales stats and simultaneously reviewing the proposed outline for the magazine show. He was meeting with Parker, Dion and Savian in about fifteen minutes and wanted to make sure he was clear on all the aspects they needed to discuss. There weren't many. Savian had done a great job outlining a show that echoed the pages of *Infinity* while expanding their popular areas.

Regan would have time to feature any red-carpet spotlights as well as tidbits on local, up-and-coming designers. Savian had suggested they not focus too much on CK Designs during the magazine show, since Regan and Camille were already working together on the reality show. Tate's segment would come at the end, with her actually inviting the writer of one of her advice letters to the show for a face-to-face therapy session.

With that, his thoughts turned to the woman who'd been sharing his bed, his living space, and his life. Sean always knew he'd settle down one day and build a family of his own. He hadn't imagined that day would come so soon, but he wasn't the type of man to fight the inevitable. He was in love with Tate Dennison and her beautiful daughter. Holding Briana in his arms, watching her sleep, and seeing her enjoy her dinner and play with toys he'd bought her gave Sean a joy he'd never felt before. No, she wasn't his blood daughter, but that didn't stop him from feeling protective and nurturing toward her. His mother had noticed the same thing when they'd returned from the police station late Sunday evening.

"She looks good on you," Janean had told him.

She'd come up behind him when he was collecting Briana's diaper bag and the dishes they'd bought for her.

"She's a great baby. Hardly ever cries," had been his simple reply.

"And her mother? Is she great, too?"

Janean had been watching him closely, and Sean recognized the "I'll be quiet and let you figure it out" stance his mother had. It was one she used with him often, most likely because she knew he would think long and hard enough to do just that.

"Yeah, she's great, too."

She nodded. "And what do you intend to do about these two great girls who've appeared in your life?"

He paused then, diaper bag on his shoulder, stuffed animal in his hand. He'd thought of this last night as he'd held Tate in his arms, thought about what the future held for them. Of course, Tate had reservations—he knew that right off the bat. She'd say they were moving too fast, that she'd been burned before, that they should take things slow. And he could counter each and every argument with one of his own and probably come out successful. But this morning as they'd shared breakfast, he'd realized something. He didn't just want to get Tate because he was a Donovan and Donovan men always got what they wanted. No, what he desired from this woman was so much deeper than that. He wanted Tate to be as ready for him as he was. He wanted her to fall in love with him in her own time, on her own terms.

"I intend to let her figure out what she wants to do about me," he said to his mother.

She'd chuckled in response. "You've already given that a lot of thought, I presume."

He smiled back. "You know me."

His mother had taken his face in her palms. He'd bent down so it would be easier when she kissed his lips with a loud smack, the way she used to when he was younger. "I know you very well, son. You're such a good man."

So his mother approved of his method. Sean only hoped Tate did, too.

"Daydreaming?" Savian said, coming into his office.

"Thinking," was Sean's friendly retort.

"Figures," his cousin said as he headed straight for the conference table across from Sean's desk.

Sean started gathering his papers and stood. He grabbed a pen out of the holder on the end of his desk as he walked to the table as well.

Savian went to the small refrigerator and pulled out a bottled water. He did a double-take at the bottles of fruit juice Sean had stashed in there and gave Sean a quizzical stare. Sean knew what he was thinking and decided not to voluntarily address it. If Savian wanted to know, he'd have to ask.

"Pass me an orange juice," he said instead.

With a seldom-heard chuckle, Savian tossed him a plastic bottle. Sean caught it, opened it and took a swallow before sitting down.

"She's domesticating you," Savian said when he'd finally taken his seat.

"What are you talking about? I've always been the

most domestic of the bunch. You guys are the ones stuck in perpetual bachelorhood."

"Hey, I resent that comment, even though I wasn't here to participate in the beginning of the conversation," Parker said as he came in with his usual jovial demeanor. His sunglasses were propped on top of his head, his suit jacket probably thrown somewhere in his office. White dress-shirt sleeves were rolled up to his elbow and his tie was crooked, as if he'd been tugging at it just before he came in. Even though Parker received compliments for how he looked in a suit, he'd never liked dressing up, ever. So the minute he could get out of dress clothes, he was peeling them off, like a kid.

"He's got fruit juice in his refrigerator," Savian said with a smirk.

Parker shook his head. "He's always been a problem. That's why I go to his house to raid his fridge all the time. He's like our mothers in a male body."

Sean frowned. "I don't think I like that statement."

"You shouldn't," Dion chimed in as he entered the office and closed the door. "It makes you sound like a ninny."

The men chuckled, feeling their closeness as they all gathered around the table. When there was a board meeting they sat with their fathers at the heads of the table and with Regan tossed somewhere in the middle. But this planning session was only for them. They'd handle it from here and then present to the board as a united front. It worked every time.

An hour and a half later, they'd ironed out all the kinks in the program's schedule and were just about to order themselves a late lunch of pizza. Which lead to one of their greatest recurring debates.

"No onions or anchovies," Dion said adamantly.

"Man, you're such a punk. What's pizza without the works?" Parker retorted.

Savian shook his head. "I have another meeting this evening. I don't want to smell like pizza-parlor funk when I go. Onions and anchovies are sick, Parker."

"Extra cheese," was Sean's only recommendation. He was cool with most of the other toppings. Besides, there was no need to chime in about the onions and anchovies, because they never won out anyway.

The sound of his door almost being knocked off its hinges silenced all four of the guys. Then there was a loud buzzing from his desk phone.

"Mr. Donovan, Ms. Dennison is here. She says it's an emergency," Gayle announced through the intercom.

Sean was up and out of his seat in seconds, going to the door to wrench it open. Tate all but fell into his arms. The first thing he noticed, besides the fact that she was out of breath, was that she was crying. His entire body clenched at the sight, fury bubbling raw inside.

"What's the matter?" he asked, cupping her face in his hands.

"It's Briana." She shook her head, tears steadily streaming. "They can't find her! She's gone, Sean! Gone!"

Dion, Savian and Parker had already come from the table to see what was going on.

"What do you mean she's gone?" Dion asked.

She didn't even look at them, she couldn't. All she could hear was the sound of the day-care principal's shaking voice through the phone as she told Tate that her baby had gone missing from their outing to the park.

"She's gone. Gone," she said, and she would have crumpled right to the floor if Sean hadn't caught her.

Chapter 19

The Big House had been set up as their central location. It was the only place where all the family could gather as they waited for news.

Devlin, who had been watching the building where Sean and Tate worked, was angry beyond words at the man he'd assigned to watch Briana at the day care. The guy had been absolutely useless—he'd been sitting in his car on his cell phone when Briana was taken. Needless to say, the guy wouldn't be working for Devlin or D&D Investigations anymore, nor anyplace else in the United States for that matter.

The day-care workers had been questioned relentlessly, first by Sean and Tate, then by Devlin—which was not a pretty sight in the least—and finally by the local police. They hadn't seen anything. It was official that when they found Briana, she would not be returning to that facility for child care.

Janean was in a state when they'd told her about Briana. She'd attempted to mask her worry with a continual rant about subpar child care in the state and across the country. Sean feared that when this was all over there'd be a Donovan Day Care somewhere with Janean spearheading the effort.

As for Tate, she sat in the same spot in the sunroom he'd guided her to two hours ago. She wouldn't drink, wouldn't eat, didn't talk, didn't even look at anyone. Her gaze stayed transfixed on the window, on the pool and the grass outside, where Briana had just played yesterday.

"Patrick Dennison is still locked up tight," Devlin said.

He stood in the doorway of the room, his all-black attire and brooding looks fitting perfectly with the somber mood. Last night, before the police appearance, the mood had been festive, communal so Devlin had blended into the background but was ever watchful.

Sean thought with a sigh that maybe he should have had Devlin stay with Briana. He and Tate could have taken the other, less attentive guard. But that was a futile thought, just as guilt was a useless emotion. There had been no reason to fear for Briana's safety. They'd thought Tate was the target, or more likely some object in Tate's apartment. Who would have ever considered that Briana might be pulled into this?

"We should expect a ransom note soon," Savian said. In his hands he held a piping-hot cup of coffee. He sat in a chair just across from where Tate had taken up residence. His gaze rested on her more times than Sean could count, which meant his cousin was worried. He wanted to reach out, to extend his comfort, but Savian wasn't good with emotions, so he just stayed close instead.

"What makes you think that?" Regan asked. She wore tight black pants today, a fuchsia-embossed tunic that came to her thighs and mile-high black boots. Her hair was pulled back into a tight ponytail that stretched to her buttocks with the added hair. Her makeup was flawless, but for the frown on her face. She stood near the window about four feet from where Tate was looking outside.

"She works for the Donovans, is living with a Donovan. It's got to be about money," Savian said simply.

Lyra shook her head. "Not everything's about money." Her reply was soft, almost as if she herself didn't believe those words.

"But Dennison is looking for something. He came back here because he said Tate had something of his. What if he had someone take Briana as some sort of blackmail plot?" Dion asked.

Bruce had been standing near his wife at the sink. Janean acted as if she were perfectly fine and did not need any support. But Sean knew better, and he kept a watchful eye on his mother as he sat next to Tate.

Uncle Reggie cleared his throat and scratched the back of his head. He'd recently cut his salt-and-pepper hair very close because the front had begun receding. He still looked sharp in his perfectly creased brown dress slacks and lightweight beige sweater.

"I don't know that this Dennison character sounds smart enough to pull off a kidnapping. Especially since he's in jail. He sounds more impulsive and prone to mess up than someone intelligent enough to orchestrate something like this."

Devlin nodded. "I agree. This had to be perfectly planned. Someone knew the day care would go on this outing. They knew when they'd be at the park and when Briana would most likely be alone for the taking."

There was a loud clanking as one of the coffee cups Janean was drying slipped out of her hand and fell into the stainless-steel sink. "Who leaves a two-year-old alone? That's just ridiculous. It's reprehensible! They should be fired or…or…shot!" she yelled finally.

And that's when Tate broke down.

With a gasp, she lowered her head, her shoulders shuddering with the intensity of the tears that broke free. Sean put his arm around her, pulled her to him and whispered in her ear.

"We'll find her, baby. If it's the last thing I do, we'll find her."

But his words were only partial consolation. Tate wanted her daughter in her arms right this moment. She wanted to smell the sweet scent of baby powder as she cuddled her close, wanted to feel the growing weight of Briana's body in her arms as she carried her to bed. She wanted to wipe more food splatters from the floor and the high chair and smile as she listened to Briana's infectious laughter.

Sitting here doing nothing wasn't helping. It was torture, and she felt like breaking through that window and running outside to call out to her daughter. But Briana wouldn't hear her, Tate knew this. She wouldn't hear her mother's voice calling her name because she didn't know where her mother was. Her daughter was with a stranger, probably scared and hungry or wet and just as uncomfortable as Tate was right now.

Her heart pounded in slow, useless beats, and she heaved and gushed on Sean's shoulder. She'd been doing this on and off since she'd gotten the call. There had been no question that she'd go to Sean. Her feet had taken to the stairs at work like lightning as she'd forgone the elevator. Gayle, Sean's assistant, had looked almost afraid to talk to her when she'd turned the corner to where Sean's office was. And when she'd gone right past her without saying a word to bang on his locked door, the poor woman had almost fainted.

He'd pulled her into his arms then, just as he was doing now, and she felt the warmth of him so close, the steady beat of his heart, the rock-solid form his presence signified. She could lean on him, and she did. When she couldn't stand, he picked her up. Now, when words failed her, he held her and said what she needed to hear, even if they were words neither of them could promise.

"Lord, help us," Janean said from across the room, her own tears breaking her down. Bruce had stood there for a reason, and he pulled his wife into his arms.

Sniffles erupted throughout the room, but Tate couldn't see who they came from. All around were people who cared, who wanted Briana back safely just as Tate did. It seemed like eons since she'd felt this type of undying support. Her heart was heavy with that realization as well.

When it was all too much, she pushed away from Sean and struggled to stand. He stood with her, his hand on the small of her back.

"I need some air," she said, looking up at him through blurry eyes. "Walk with me."

It hadn't been a burden to ask. And just like when she'd gone to his office, there'd been no second thought. She couldn't be alone. And why should she be when he was near?

He held her hand and walked her out of the room. They used the door where Devlin stood, and she watched him give Sean a nod. That probably meant he'd be right behind them, but Tate couldn't bring herself to think about that. Her mind was full of much more important things.

Sean seemed to have a destination as he led her past the swimming pool, down a small incline to the wooden planks of what looked like their own private dock. When they stopped walking, he wrapped his arms around her from behind, leaning forward to whisper in her ear.

"I'm so sorry this is happening. But I promise you I'll do everything in my power to get her back."

"I believe you," she said with a sigh. "I mean, I really do believe you. And I haven't believed what came out of a man's mouth for a while now."

"I'm not any other man, Tate."

She shook her head. "You definitely do not have to tell me that. I've never known anyone like you."

There was a cool breeze blowing off the water as the sun set behind them. Tate turned in his arms, letting her forehead rest on his chest for a moment. He rubbed up and down her back, holding her close. She felt so safe, so protected, and she yearned for her baby to feel the same way.

"I'm glad we met," she said softly, looking up at him. "I'm so glad that your cousin wanted to add me to the show or else you probably never would have come to my office. I'm glad we went to dinner and that you came when my apartment was broken into. You're always saving me," she said with a broken chuckle. "And I'm glad."

"I wish this wasn't happening to you," he told her.

"Sean, I just want her back. If it's Patrick, he can have everything in that damned apartment. I just want my baby back."

"I want her back, too. And if it's Patrick, he's not getting a damned thing. But maybe my fist in his face again. My cousin has all the investigators in their Connecticut office working on this. We're going to find her and we're going to get the bastards that did this. They're going to be sorry they ever messed with you."

She shook her head. "No, they're going to be sorry they ever messed with a Donovan."

Chapter 20

"I don't care if you text him or email him or shout it off the damned rooftop!" she yelled. "Just get me my money!"

This was one crazy sistah, Butch thought with a frown as he walked out of the room and resisted the urge to slam the door shut behind him. But like her, he needed the money, too. His old lady was having their fourth child, and funds had been tight for the past couple of months. So tight they were being evicted next Monday morning if he didn't come up with three months' back rent plus grocery money.

A dude in jail had offered him three thousand, cash, if he took this kid and brought her to this address. Now this crazy chick was freakin' out every ten seconds because the kid was crying and this wasn't her responsibility and all this other BS.

Butch just wanted his cash.

But now that he'd had a moment to register the full situation, he figured that three thousand might be farther away than it was yesterday at this time when he was sitting at home playing spades with his homeboys.

He was getting too old for this crap, is what he was thinking as he pulled out his cell phone and punched in the number she'd given him. Butch had no idea who he was texting. He just assumed that this person was the kid's parent and would pay whatever or do whatever psycho-chick in there wanted to get her child back.

So he typed in the message:

U want ur daughter? Meet me at 212 Lemoncage Way at midnight. Bring the key.

He had no idea what that meant, but he prayed it meant that his three thousand was only a few hours away from being in his hands. If not, and his old lady found out that he still didn't have any money, Butch was going to be better off in jail for kidnapping.

"No. It's out of the question," Tate said adamantly. "She's my daughter, so I'm the one who's going."

Sean wanted to yell back that she was "their" daughter, but he didn't. He knew it was too sensitive of a time to bring up how badly he wanted them to be a family. He recognized that Tate was in a very precarious state right now; she was crying one minute, trying to be upbeat the next, and he was going to respect that. But what he wasn't going to have was her thinking he would be some kind of punk and sit back while Briana was out there in the hands of some deranged kidnapper.

"I don't know this number, Tate. But anyone can get my work cell number off our website, and whoever it is has Briana," he told her seriously.

They were all back in the sunroom again, the dark evening sky making it necessary to turn on the inside lights. Janean had fixed a huge pot of chicken and rice and a jug of iced tea. Nobody was really in the mood to eat, but nobody was brave enough to tell Janean that either, so they ate.

That was about an hour ago. Ten minutes ago, Sean had received the text.

"Or they want you to think they have Briana," Dion said. "What if it's a false alarm?"

"We haven't made any statements about Briana being missing. How would anyone else even know I was involved, unless they really had her?" Sean asked.

"But what's this about a key?" Bruce asked. "Do you have any type of key?"

He was looking at Tate, which was making her more than a little nervous. But she cleared her throat and answered, "No. I don't know about any key."

"I'm going," Sean said adamantly. "It's eleven-thirty now. Lemoncage is at least twenty minutes away."

"We need to leave now. I have two unmarked cars that are going to meet us there," Devlin said solemnly and then reached into his pocket. "Here, take this."

Sean took the key from his hand.

"Right, that's going to work," Regan said skeptically. "What if they want to try it out first? And what if your betrayal makes them mad and they shoot you or something?"

"Regan!" Caroline admonished her daughter as Janean dabbed at tearful eyes.

Regan crossed her arms over her chest. "I'm just covering all the bases."

"She's right. That's why you shouldn't go," Tate said. "This isn't your battle."

Bruce walked to her and put a hand on her shoulder. "I know you don't know us all that well yet, but my boys protect what's theirs, no matter what the cost. He's not going to back down, and unfortunately, honey, you're gonna have to learn how to sit back and worry with the other womenfolk."

He smiled at her and wrapped his arm around her shoulders.

"He's right," Lyra chimed in. "They're a stubborn bunch. He's never going to listen to you. Best to just quit while you're ahead."

"Besides, I'm going with him. And Devlin and his backup will be there, too," Dion said, going to stand beside Sean.

"Who said you were coming?" Sean asked.

Dion just shook his head. "You don't even want to waste time arguing this with me."

He was right. Sean didn't want to waste any more time. He wanted to go get Briana. So he crossed the room to Tate. He took her out of his father's protective grip and pulled her in for a tight hug. In her ear he whispered, "I'm going to bring our little girl home. Trust me."

She didn't respond right away and just kept her stubborn fists clenched at his chest, her head looking down. He said it again. "Trust me?"

After a few silent moments she nodded.

"Look at me," he told her.

She did, and in her eyes Sean saw his future. Marriage, a house, a lavishly decorated bedroom for Briana and another child's bedroom for the baby they would make together.

"I love you and Briana. I'm not going to lose my family when I've just found them. We have too much to do together."

Her eyes pooled with tears, and her bottom lip trembled. Sean leaned in to kiss those lips. "Trust me?"

She nodded immediately. "I trust you."

"I don't trust this guy," Dion said the minute Devlin's black Hummer came to a stop at the corner of 212 Lemoncage.

"We don't need to trust him. I just want to get Briana," Sean said adamantly.

"That's the goal here," Devlin told him. "Get him to bring out Briana. You need proof that she's alive and well. Then exchange her for the key."

Dion shook his head. "I've got to agree with Regan, which isn't always a good practice. But what if he wants to test the key out?"

"I'll cross that bridge when I get to it," Sean said, stepping out of the car.

212 Lemoncage was a residential house. It was a split level that had been painted bright pink with white trimming. All of the windows were covered by bars, which gave Sean a sick and claustrophobic feeling. When they stepped up to the doorway, he wasn't surprised to see that the screen door was made from the same bars that covered the windows. He turned a cracked gold knob and pulled the door open. When he felt Dion take the weight of the screened door from him, he knocked. For

endless moments there was no answer. Then the door was cracked.

"You're not alone," a man Sean could barely see called out in a gruff voice.

"No. I'm not. You didn't say to come alone."

The man cursed. "All right, but I don't have no weapons, so you don't bring none in with you."

Sean looked over his shoulder to Dion, who shrugged. He figured they were both thinking how stupid this guy had to be to think that by just telling them not to bring in any weapons they would listen. Even though Sean and Dion were licensed to carry a gun and they had trained at the firing range for years, they didn't have weapons on them. Devlin did have a gun in his waistband, but he was sitting in the truck listening through the receiver he'd taped to Sean's chest. Any type of taped confession could get the kidnapper put away for a good while, so Devlin had said.

The door opened with a creak that reminded Sean of an old haunted house. He scanned the surroundings the moment he was inside. It was dim, lit only by a candle in the far corner of what was probably the living room. Through the archway straight ahead he saw there were no lights on in that room either. His guess was that there was no electricity, or at the very least no air conditioning, because the air was thick and muggy inside.

"Where is she?" Dion asked the second the door closed.

There was a sniffing sound, and through the shadows Sean could see the guy using his arm to wipe his nose. He appeared disheveled from head to toe, and

Sean only hoped he hadn't put those grimy hands on Briana.

"I'm supposed to get the key first," he said, his voice slurred a bit.

"He's high as hell," Dion said with disgust. Sean knew his tone of voice linked back to Lyra's mother, who had been addicted to drugs and had died in a car crash a few months ago.

"I'll give you the key when I see that Briana's all right," Sean spoke calmly. If this guy was high on drugs, maybe that could be their advantage.

There were two of them and only one of him. He didn't have a gun in his hand, and Sean prayed there wasn't someone with a loaded weapon just beyond one of these dark rooms.

"Just let me see her," he continued. "Then I'll give you the key and we all can go about our business."

"I want the key first," the man said.

Dion took a step toward the man and Sean moved beside him, putting a hand on his arm. He knew what his brother was thinking and figured he'd give it one last try before this meeting turned physical.

"I want my daughter, *now*," he said in a voice louder and with more conviction than just a few seconds ago.

"Then come and get her," a female voice said from behind the man.

He knew that voice, despised it, but he knew it. Sean turned slowly to see Briana's tear-filled eyes illuminated by another candle that was held too close to her face for safety. The woman was holding her. Long black hair had been pulled back into a ponytail, and the face was flawless. Large dark eyes stared at him below elegantly arched eyebrows. Her lips were glossed, the only way he'd ever seen them, as they spread into a smile.

"Sabine," he whispered, a sick feeling spreading in his gut.

"Trent?"

"Sabine Ravenell is really Sarah Ann Dennison. She changed her name when she did her first adult movie seventeen years ago. She's one of two children born to Darlene and Joel Dennison in Daytona Beach, Florida. Her younger brother is—"

Devlin cut him off. "Patrick Dennison."

"Bingo!" Trent said through the other line.

"Damn it!" he cursed.

"What's up? This cracks both cases. Sabine doesn't have enough money to meet the price she bid for *Infinity,* but I see her brother's been racking up some funds, probably through his continued fraud empire. He makes Madoff look like a saint."

"Sean and Dion went into the house to meet the kidnapper."

"You sent them in alone?" The question came with a low rumble in Trent's voice. Devlin knew that wasn't a good sign.

"Relax. I'm right outside, and I've got backup not ten seconds away. But they're not expecting Sabine Ravenell."

It was Trent's turn to curse. "She's not just a porn star, Dev. One of her managers was found dead three years ago in L.A. They always suspected her but didn't have enough evidence to make an arrest. She's a killer, and you sent my cousins in there alone."

Devlin was already getting out of the SUV. He had

his Bluetooth in one ear, the earpiece that linked him to his backup partners in the other. "I'm on it," he said into the Bluetooth and disconnected it before Trent could really go off.

"Cover the house!" he yelled to his backup through the earpiece.

He didn't hear them get out of their cars or hit the ground running, but he knew they did. It was what they were trained to do. Devlin was first at the front door. Only a shadow caught in his peripheral said he had backup right behind him.

Things seemed to move in extra slow motion inside the house.

Sean took steps toward Sabine the moment he saw it was her. Without a word, he reached for Briana. Sabine swung away so he couldn't reach her. The action caused the candle to fall to the floor. He didn't think to grab it; his only focus was getting his baby girl.

"All you had to do was sign over the damned magazine!" she yelled at him.

She was taking a few steps away, like she was prepared to run, but Sean was not about to let her take off. He reached out and grabbed a handful of her ponytail, wrapping it around his hand and using it as a sort of leash to pull her back, stopping her in her tracks.

She yelled and Briana started to cry.

"Give me my daughter!"

"She's not your baby, you naive idiot! She's my niece!" Sabine screamed at him.

Sean heard her words but didn't have time to process them. When he had her close enough, he yanked on her hair so hard that her head jerked back and she yelled again. She reached up to swipe her nails over his face, in the process releasing her hold on Briana. He instantly grabbed his baby and cradled her close. He felt the sting of her nails making contact with his face and then pushed Sabine to the ground with a shoulder bump.

"Get your crazy ass away from her!" he yelled, turning to run toward Dion and the front of the house.

Sabine could stay here with the grungy guy. They were leaving. His heart beat wildly against his chest as he held Briana close, rubbing a hand over her head and whispering to her as he went.

Suddenly he saw flames and almost stepped right into a wall of sparking orange and yellow heat. Instinctively, he grabbed at the shirt Briana was wearing, lifting it from the bottom to pull over her head so she wouldn't inhale the smoke. He didn't know the layout of the house and wasn't sure how to get around the wall of flames. As soon as he decided to go to the right he heard the gunshot. Seconds later he felt the burn of a hot bullet ripping through his flesh.

It took everything in him—all the love he felt for this little girl in his arms, for the woman waiting for him to return, for his mother and his father, for his brother who had been so loyal and dedicated to come with him—all of it created an adrenaline rush that pushed him forward. His legs moved without any real direction from him. His baby gripped his shirt, her wails growing louder and louder.

He couldn't get enough air in his lungs. He smelled the stench of burning flesh, but he kept moving and moving until he couldn't move anymore and he fell to the ground, dampness covering his face with a stinging sensation.

Briana still cried, which meant she was alive and she was safe. Lights flashed, blue and red. A siren sounded. Police, he thought. Then he coughed.

"Tate," her name fell from his lips before everything around him went black.

Chapter 21

Tate sat in a different chair now. It wasn't as comfortable as the one she'd been in all night, and the surroundings weren't as warm, but she didn't dare move. Nobody could get her out of this room. Nor could they convince her to let the hospital bassinet, which was too small for Briana, out of her sight. She was staying right here where she could see her baby. She could reach out and touch her, feel her pulse and know that she was still alive.

Sean had been rushed into surgery before she'd arrived at the hospital early this morning. They said he'd lost a lot of blood, that the bullet had entered through his back and was stuck somewhere in his chest. Briana had been rushed to the pediatric unit, where she was being checked out for smoke inhalation.

Lyra and Regan walked with her to the pediatric unit,

one on either side of her. As she'd waited to see Briana, all sorts of scenarios had run through her mind. There was a fire and talk of some woman named Sabine being there and an unknown man who had died. Tate wanted to take comfort in the fact that Briana was alive, which was a tremendous blessing, considering all that had gone on. Still, her legs shook and her hands trembled when she finally walked into the room.

Briana had a tiny tube up her nose, but she was sitting up, a light yellow hospital gown with clowns all over it hanging from her shoulder. She had smudges on her cheeks and her eyes looked red, but as Tate drew closer her precious baby lifted her small arms up in the air to her. Tate rushed forward and scooped her up in her arms. Tears poured from Tate's eyes as she held Briana in her arms and felt the beat of Briana's heartbeat against her chest. Joy had soared through her with a gush of breath that she hadn't realized she'd been holding.

Regan and Lyra both hugged Briana, and they all stood around her cooing and kissing for what seemed like forever.

Then, as if on cue, a cloud passed over the early morning sun. The room grew darker, colder, and Tate gasped, "Sean."

It had taken some convincing and the Donovan name being tossed around—Tate was sure—for the pediatric doctors to allow her to take Briana to another floor of the hospital. They called upstairs ahead of time so the trauma unit would not be alarmed by seeing her with the bassinet and baby in tow.

For an endless amount of time they'd sat in the waiting room. Waiting.

Dion had been treated for smoke inhalation as well. He and the man that had allegedly kidnapped Briana had gotten into a fight and crashed right into Devlin and his men as they had entered the house. It had taken a few minutes to untangle the men and discover that Sean wasn't there. By the time the discovery was made, they all smelled smoke. And only seconds later they heard the gunshot. By that time the house had filled with smoke and they couldn't get to Sean. They'd run out of the front of the house to keep from being engulfed in the flames and smoke, when Devlin heard the call of one of his men at the back of the house, where Sean had made his getaway.

They'd found him lying on the grass, blood pouring from his back, Briana on her knees beside him crying.

"He made it through the surgery, and we were able to remove the bullet," the doctor said the moment he walked through the swinging double doors.

"He'll be in recovery for another couple of hours, then we'll move him to a room."

"I have to see him," Tate said.

She'd been standing behind the Donovans, letting his parents and his brother be the first to get the news. But she couldn't remain quiet, and her feet shifted from side to side as her hand stayed on the bassinet.

"Can I see him now?" she asked anxiously.

Janean Donovan moved through the family members to come to Tate's side. Tate wondered nervously what she would say.

"Yes, she needs to see him," she said, putting an arm around Tate. "He'll want to know that Briana is safe."

Tate didn't know what to say, but she found herself doing something she never thought she'd do—leaning into Janean's embrace for strength.

She'd decided after Patrick that she'd never lean on anyone again. That she and Briana were in this life alone. And then she'd come to Miami and found this family, who had welcomed her with open arms. She didn't know what to say to express how grateful she was and figured it probably wasn't the time to go into all her revelations about relationships.

Instead, when the doctor nodded his head, Tate pushed the bassinet ahead of her through the double doors. Down a long corridor she traveled with the doctor right beside her.

"This is highly unusual. Children aren't even allowed in the trauma ward, let alone back here in intensive care. But I know this has been a trying night for everyone. Still, you have to make this quick. When he's moved to his room, I'll make sure you and the baby can stay in there with him."

He was a nice-looking guy, with his honey-blond hair that curled around his ears and clear blue eyes. What was nicer was the tone of his voice, the soft baritone that reassured her the more he spoke.

"Thank you very much," she said when they came to a room at the end of the hall.

The doctor opened the door for her and she walked in with the bassinet. She stopped at the end of the bed and simply stared down at Sean, who was surrounded by machines and white sheets. His chest was bare but for the bright white bandages, and his hands were still at his sides.

"Sean." She said his name so quietly she didn't think he'd even hear her. She'd barely heard herself.

But his eyes opened. They closed languidly, then opened again.

"Tate."

Her name was a whisper on his lips, a gravelly sound that she barely recognized. She went to him then, lifting his hand in hers.

"I'm so sorry. I'm so sorry I brought this into your life. I wish it were me. I swear I wish it were me instead of you."

She lifted his fingers to hers and kissed them.

"Briana," he whispered next.

"She's fine." Tate moved back to the bassinet and lifted Briana out.

She was asleep, and her head fell instantly against Tate's shoulder. But when Tate got closer to Sean he lifted his hand to touch Briana. She leaned close to him to make it easier. His fingers rubbed the baby's back, over her mussed hair.

"You saved her," Tate told him. "You carried her right out of that house away from the kidnappers and the fire."

Tears poured down her cheeks as she spoke. "I owe you everything, Sean. Everything. How can I ever repay you for saving my baby?"

Sean now touched the side of her face and Briana's at the same time. He'd winced when he moved the left arm across his body and she'd almost pulled away from him. But his gaze held her still.

"Marry me," he said earnestly.

He'd become blurry through her tears and his voice was raspy to her ears, but it was still Sean. She'd know his touch anywhere, this feeling that always seemed to settle over her when he was around. All of it was familiar and it was comforting. It was everything Tate had ever wanted. So her answer was no surprise.

"Yes," she said, nodding her head enthusiastically. "Yes. I'll marry you."

Sean had quickly slipped off to a deep sleep, and Tate wondered if he'd even remember his question when he awoke.

She decided that it didn't matter. She'd be here regardless.

When he'd been moved to his private room and his family had filed in to see him, they'd all been ecstatic that he was going to recover. But the pain medications had still kept him asleep.

Janean had offered to take Briana home since she was technically discharged from the hospital now, but Tate wouldn't let her. She just wasn't ready to be apart from her so soon. Janean understood and promised to return later with a change of clothes for both her and Briana.

Now it was early afternoon and Briana was up. One of the nurses had been nice enough to get her one of the leftover patient lunches. Briana wasn't a fan of the food but managed to get at least some of the tuna down. She'd eaten all of the peaches and drank the milk. Now she sat in the bassinet playing with the blankets.

There was a knock at the door.

"Hi," Devlin said, peeking his head inside.

"Hi," she replied, giving him a slight smile. She owed him a lot and had thanked him last night.

"He's still not awake?" Devlin asked, coming all the way into the room and stopping at the end of the bed.

"He comes and goes. The painkillers are really strong," she told him.

Devlin nodded and continued to watch Sean.

Here was a complex man, Tate thought as she continued to stare at Devlin. He was tall—not as tall as Sean's six feet, four inches—but still tall enough to tower over her. And he was broad—his body was solid and muscled everywhere, from the veins that bulged in his neck to the thick sculpted shape of his thighs. He wore pants that looked like parachutes that were tucked into his black steel-toed boots. His shirt almost seemed too small as it molded against his iron-man chest. When she looked at him she instantly thought wrestling star or bodybuilder.

Until she looked at his face.

He had dark brown skin, like tree bark, and even darker eyes framed by lashes that were thick and long and probably the envy of every woman who'd ever seen them. But it was his eyes that said so much more than any other aspect of his body. He wasn't happy.

For a second Tate wondered if people could look at her like this months ago and say the same thing about her. If this man's unhappiness cloaked him like a shield, she figured hers probably had, too. She wondered how she appeared now. Was there a glow of happiness surrounding her instead? Lord, she prayed so.

"You always stare at people in hospitals like that?"

The sound of Sean's voice yanked Tate from her thoughts and she looked to the bed to see that he was fully awake. He didn't look as groggy as he had earlier.

"Only when dudes act like pansies, laying in bed

like they're really injured," Devlin replied with a hearty chuckle. "How you feeling?"

"I feel like I was shot," Sean said.

Tate smiled. His voice didn't sound as raspy as it had before. When she'd asked the nurse, they'd explained that during surgery he'd been intubated and that could cause sore and raspy throats.

"You feel like hearing what's been going down since you decided to jump in front of that bullet?"

"Only if you're going to tell me they put Sabine's crazy ass in jail."

"Something like that."

Briana began making noises, lifting her arms toward Sean. She'd been wanting to get on that bed with him all day, but Tate wouldn't let her. To keep her quiet so they could all hear what Devlin had to say, she picked her up and sat her in her lap. That was a mistake. Briana wanted Sean and she wasn't letting up this time, probably because she could see that he was awake.

"Come here, pretty girl," he said, lifting one of his arms for her.

"Are you sure? I know you're still in pain," she said.

He shook his head. "I want to hold her."

Gingerly she placed Briana on the bed and watched as Sean lifted her little fingers to his lips for a kiss.

"Hey, cutie," Sean said, letting Briana touch his face, his nose, his lips.

"You can continue, Devlin," he said without looking at the man.

"Did you know your ex-husband had a sister?" he asked her.

Tate shook her head. "No. He didn't talk about his family much."

"Sabine Ravenell is his sister. It looks like she took care of him when she was riding high on the porn circuit. Put him through college because their parents were too poor to do so. When he completed college she was on the downswing and probably used a guilt trip to get him to make her some money."

"Wait a minute. Are you saying that the money he stole from my grandfather went to his sister?" Tate asked.

"That's how she bought Onyx Publications," Sean answered. "He was the investor in her new business venture."

"And he's been continuing with the fraud, even after the FBI got wind of what he was doing," Devlin told them.

Tate was astounded. "How could that be? When I talked to those agents they seemed positive they had enough information to charge and convict Patrick."

Devlin was shaking his head. "Their star witness backed out."

"Marsha," she said with a sigh. He'd probably bought her something to keep her quiet.

"Yeah, but he made a dent in a dozen retirement funds in Daytona just before showing up here. So I think they've got enough on him now. Not to mention the conspiracy-to-kidnapping and breaking-and-entering charges here. I think he's going to be locked away for a long time."

"What about Sabine?" Sean asked.

Devlin folded his arms across his chest. "Conspiracy to kidnap, assault, attempted murder. She's going to do some time as well."

"Good."

   "Yeah, now you all can live happily ever after," Devlin said with a smirk that was probably as close as the man came to a smile.

Chapter 22

2 Months Later

The best thing about their new house was the large backyard with plush green grass, mature palm trees and colorful sprays of begonias and blue daze.

Tate had told him the names of the flowers, but all Sean knew was that he loved the way the colors brightened the large space, adding a touch of whimsy to the area. They'd been here a week and he'd already purchased a swing set and sandbox for Briana. They had a grill and deck furniture sitting beneath the alcove designed for entertaining. In the garage, both their cars were parked. In one of the four bedrooms, the walls were freshly painted the lightest shade of yellow, waiting patiently for Briana's new furniture to be delivered.

In the early morning hours of this Saturday morning

Tate had already been up with Briana. Tate had been in a cleaning frenzy since they'd moved in and had decided to take the week off from work. He'd told her they could hire someone to clean the house, but she'd insisted on doing it herself. Sean was inclined to give her what she wanted.

That went for both Tate and Briana. If they asked for the moon he'd swing a lasso and pull it right out of the sky for them. That's how much he loved them.

After a quick shower he followed the noise down the hall to the room that was going to be a guest room but right now housed a lot of boxes and furniture Tate had picked up from her apartment. He stood in the doorway a few moments, just taking in the sight. Briana wore a pink-and-white polka-dot top with a ruffled bottom that capped her chubby little thighs. Her feet were bare as they slapped across the wood floor. She moved faster and faster every day, Sean thought as she raced across the room to tackle another empty box. Tate looked over her shoulder to make sure Briana hadn't hurt herself. She was very protective now and kept Briana in her sight at all times. They'd even found a new day care with the help of Sean's mother.

The new day care worked out well for Janean because it was owned by the daughter of the co-chair of one of Janean's committees. This meant Janean was allowed to drop in whenever she wanted and to take Briana for a couple hours a day after she'd checked with Sean and Tate. His mother was absolutely in love with that little girl, and Sean couldn't blame her.

A loud crashing sound pulled Sean from his thoughts, and he crossed the room quickly to help Tate with the boxes that had fallen onto the extra car seat in the corner.

"Damn it, it's broken," Tate said when Sean had pulled the boxes, which had been filled with books, to the side.

"Baby, we have new car seats. One in my car, one in yours and one at the day care. Even my mother has a car seat. It's okay if this one is broken."

Tate was lifting the seat, checking the belt and back frame.

"She can't even fit in that one anymore. It's an infant seat."

"I know," she said with a frown. "But it was a baby shower gift. The girls at the job I was at gave it to me. I figured I'd use it again someday, maybe."

She was wearing sweat pants and a tank top, and her hair was pulled up high on her head, wayward tendrils falling around her face. She looked so fresh and so pretty even after unpacking boxes.

He touched her shoulders, massaged them gently. "When we have our next baby, I'll buy us another car seat. Hell, you'll probably have a baby shower at work and my mother will no doubt orchestrate a huge production. We might end up with four more car seats." He chuckled at that thought because it was closer to the truth than Tate probably knew.

She laughed, too. "Yeah, I'm probably being silly. I'll just put this down with the trash pile."

But as she said that, her fingers slipped behind the backing of the seat.

"What's this?" she asked, pulling it out.

It was an envelope.

"Maybe a piece of mail that fell while you were packing," Sean suggested as he picked up more of the books that had fallen out of the boxes.

Tate shook her head. "No. It's not addressed."

She ripped the envelope open and looked inside. Her gasp alerted Sean, and he moved in closer. "What is it?"

Tate pulled something out of the envelope. "It's a key."

"I can't believe I forgot about the safe deposit box," Tate said that night after dinner.

Sean had cooked hot dogs and hamburgers on the grill, and Dion and Lyra had come over to join them.

"Do you remember what's in the box?" Dion asked just before emptying his bottle of beer.

"I didn't have anything of value except for the life insurance policies I took out just before I had Briana. That's the last time I went to the box," Tate said, sitting back in her chair and loving the feel of the cool night breeze on her cheeks.

"Was Patrick's name on the box as well?" Lyra asked.

She had just announced last week that she was pregnant. She looked absolutely stunning with her sun-tinted complexion and lovely hazel eyes.

Tate nodded. "Yeah, it was."

"You should go take a look," Dion suggested.

Sean reached across the table to take her hand. "I agree. We should go to Maryland and find out what's in this box. Sabine asked specifically for a key. This must be what they were looking for."

That was all the more reason Tate didn't want to be bothered with it at all. She wanted to put that chapter of her life behind her. She didn't want any parts of Patrick Dennison—none except her little girl.

But something told her she wasn't completely finished with him yet.

Chapter 23

Tate had never seen so much money in her life. Stacks and stacks of hundred-dollar bills were packed neatly in five black shoe boxes. There were also about a million dollars in bonds and paperwork describing deposits into two accounts in the Cayman Islands—the name on the accounts were that of a dummy business that Sean said must have belonged to Patrick.

This was Patrick's stash. It was the money he'd conned numerous elderly individuals out of. Finding it would be a godsend to them. That's what the FBI agent had said when Sean had contacted them a couple hours after they found the money. There was also some jewelry in the box and the agent asked her if it was hers. But it wasn't. The only thing she took from the box were the two life insurance policies she'd put in there.

Now they were back at the hotel in Maryland. They'd

left Briana in Miami with a very excited Janean, since they were returning in the morning. Tonight, Sean had said he had a surprise for her.

She'd dressed in a peach dress that hugged her curves and made her feel very feminine. He was dressed in a black suit and yellow tie, and she felt like royalty as they were led to the very back of the hotel's premier restaurant. They were seated at a table that had more chairs than they needed.

He hadn't said a word about the impromptu proposal he'd offered when he'd been in the hospital. That seemed like ages ago, and Tate refused to bring it up. She'd agreed to move into the house with him because it was good for Briana, and she was in love with him. If she had to wait for a real proposal, that would be fine. She was confident it would come eventually.

With a ready smile, she sat at the table and gazed at the menu. Really, she wasn't reading a thing on there. She didn't care what she ate, as long as she ate enough not to be lightheaded for this special night.

Their table was right next to a large window that looked out onto the Chesapeake Bay. It was the height of crabbing season, so several boats could be seen pulling in for the day. She remembered watching the crabbers bring in their catch and then selling the crabs to the local merchants down at the pier. Every now and then, one of the fishermen they were friendly with would give her and Blake a couple of crabs and they'd take them home for grandpa to steam.

It hit her at that moment that she was back home in Maryland. Her grandfather's house was about an hour away from where they were staying, but this was the closest she'd been to home in years. That thought was bittersweet.

"What would you like to drink?" The waitress had come to the table and was addressing Tate.

Before she could answer, a familiar voice said, "A tall half-and-half with plenty of ice."

Tate turned around in her chair so fast she almost fell out of it. She whispered his name as she stood. "Grandpa."

"Get over here and hug me, gal," he said, lifting his big, beefy arms.

Tate did as she was told. She'd always done as Grandpa said, until the fateful day when he'd warned her about Patrick.

When he wrapped those hefty arms around her she cried, because there was nothing else she could do. He always called her "gal," her and Blake and Jamie—he called them all that no matter what.

"Turn her loose, Dad. Let somebody else get a hug."

That was her father, and she couldn't get into his arms fast enough. Her heart slammed against her chest as the smell of his Old Spice cologne permeated her nostrils. "Daddy, I missed you so much."

"Then you shouldn't have stayed away," Charlie Griffin said, patting her on the top of her head and letting his fingers trickle over her face until he could nip her chin.

Just as he did when she was little.

Behind him was Blake dressed in black capris and a flared top and Jamie wearing her signature jeans, tennis shoes and T-shirt with some odd saying printed on the front. Her sisters.

The reunion was teary, and the waitress quickly

brought everyone tall glasses of half lemonade and half iced tea. They sipped and talked until baskets of hush puppies, fried calamari and bowls of crab soup were situated in front of them.

"If this boy of yours hadn't called me, we wouldn't have even known you were here," her grandfather said.

Sean had been quiet, watching her and her family, reaching out to take her hand underneath the table.

"You called my grandfather?" Tate asked, turning to him.

Sean shrugged. "Figured since we were here, it would be rude to not see everyone. And you know how my mother is about me being rude."

"Good mama you got then," Grandpa said, popping a hush puppy into his mouth.

Tate took a spoonful of soup and savored the tangy flavor of the Old Bay seasoning.

"He also told us about that reprobate you married," Blake added. "I had a few of those families he robbed in Daytona call me at the Legal Aid Bureau."

Blake was an attorney and worked a lot with pro bono cases on the East Coast. Jamie was a gym teacher, which was not at all a surprise, since their father had her in every sport there was when she was growing up.

Tate sighed. "I was wrong. I shouldn't have let him keep me away from you guys." She figured that was the admission they all wanted to hear, so she wasn't about to make them wait for it.

Her father waved a hand. "You were in love. People do crazy things when they're in love."

"Yeah, like call his girlfriend's family and plan a surprise get-together," Sean said before taking another gulp of his half and half.

"Actually, I think that was kind of cute," Jamie added.

Blake smiled. "Very smart of you to make that call. Then again, I've heard the Donovans are a pretty smart bunch."

"Oh, you've heard of us?" Sean asked.

Blake nodded. "Your cousin Ben and I shared a mutual federal detainee about a year ago. We had to communicate regarding who would get the scum bag in their courtroom first. He won, since he works defense, but if he got his client out of jail, I'd get next shot at hanging him."

Sean laughed. Tate knew that Ben Donovan was Sean's cousin from Las Vegas. She'd learned a lot about the Donovans in the time she'd been with Sean.

Dinner continued with steamed lobster, soft-shell crab sandwiches, crab cake sandwiches and fried chicken platters. And when they were all stuffed and probably ready to doze off, Sean stood.

"I asked you all here because I wanted Tate to reconnect with her family. I'm happy she's had the opportunity to do so."

He spoke like he was a politician making a grand speech for re-election. Strong, confident, authoritative. Tate loved to hear him talk this way.

"But I also wanted to kill two birds with one stone," he continued, reaching into his suit jacket pocket and pulling out a small box.

Blake gasped. Charlie put both his elbows up on the table and stared with a questioning look. Grandpa fake coughed, hiding a grin. And Jamie glowed like she'd been the one to orchestrate this entire scenario.

As for Tate, she didn't know what to do. Once she'd

seen her grandfather, she'd figured that he was the surprise Sean had for her. But she should have known better.

"Mr. Griffin, I'd like to ask for permission to marry your daughter," he said, turning to look at Charlie.

"He's got good eyes," Grandpa tried to whisper to Charlie, but the entire table heard him loud and clear.

Charlie nodded. "I've seen his eyes, Dad." Charlie nodded and kept looking at Sean.

"You know that fool hurt her before," Charlie said.

"Yes, sir, I do," Sean said.

"You wouldn't be planning to do the same would you?"

Sean shook his head. "No, sir. I can promise you my goal will be to make her the happiest woman alive."

Charlie nodded. "That's a good goal to have. But you see, she's my daughter, so I know that might be a pretty steep mountain you're trying to climb."

Blake and Jamie both laughed.

"I'm up for the challenge," Sean said.

"I think you are," Charlie said, scratching at his beard. "I believe you are. So I give you my permission. But now that I know who your family is, I know where to come with my rifle if I so much as see one tear in her eye because of you."

"Yes, sir," Sean said.

He pushed his chair back and lowered himself to one knee in front of Tate.

"I asked you this before, in my hospital room. I thought I heard you say yes, but then you never started planning any wedding. I figured it was because you were waiting for a ring. So I'm going to do this again, but right this time."

Tate was trembling all over as she extended her hand to Sean. Her eyes watered so that his face was a blur in front of her. But his eyes, they were clear, and she locked in on them and felt all the love she had for this man come rushing to the surface.

"I think I've loved you since that first day in your office. I know I loved Briana from the moment she looked up at me from her crib. I want nothing else, need nothing else in this world but you two. Please do me the tremendous honor of becoming my wife."

She could do this, Tate thought. She could open her mouth and speak, had been doing it for years. Her lips actually moved, but nothing came out. Tears dripped down onto her cheeks as he put the biggest, clearest diamond she'd ever seen onto her left ring finger. When words still weren't coming, she simply nodded. And nodded. And nodded.

Sean smiled, lifting her up out of the chair and pulling her into a tight hug. When his lips touched hers, she quickly acquiesced. There was no longer a need for words.

* * * * *

When it comes to matchmaking, will two longtime friends put their relationship on the line for the sake of love?

ESSENCE BESTSELLING AUTHOR
ADRIANNE BYRD

For ten years, lawyer Destiny Brockman saw her carefree—but very, very fine—neighbor Miles Stafford as just a good friend. So when she declares that there are no good men in Atlanta, Miles proposes a friendly wager: to set each other up on a date with the perfect match. But could the undeniable attraction that's been simmering between them for years bring the sweetest reward!

Available October 2012 wherever books are sold!

REQUEST YOUR FREE BOOKS!

2 FREE NOVELS
PLUS 2 *FREE GIFTS!*

KIMANI™
ROMANCE

Love's ultimate destination!

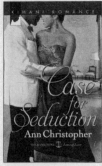 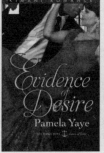 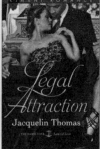

Harlequin® *Desire*

ALWAYS POWERFUL, PASSIONATE AND PROVOCATIVE.

**A BRAND-NEW WESTMORELAND
FAMILY NOVEL FROM *NEW YORK TIMES*
BESTSELLING AUTHOR**

BRENDA JACKSON

Megan Westmoreland needs answers about her
family's past. And Rico Claiborne is the man to
find them. But when the truth comes out, Rico
offers her a shoulder to lean on…and much,
much more. Megan has heard that passions burn
hotter in Texas. Now she's ready to find out….

TEXAS WILD

"Jackson's characters are…hot enough to burn the pages."
—*RT Book Reviews* on *Westmoreland's Way*

Available October 2 from Harlequin Desire®.